This book is a work of fiction. Names, characters, places, and incidents are either the works of the author's imagination or used fictitiously. Any resemblance to actual events, locals, or persons, living or dead, is entirely coincidental.

Chapter One

Wyatt James looked out the window and watched the trees, houses, and buildings pass by as the train rumbled along the track. His mind was blank. Wyatt rubbed his tired, blue eyes. He lifted his arms over his head and stretched out his 6'3" frame before relaxing his muscles. Wyatt had trouble focusing his thoughts and he frequently lost track of time. In this case, he had no idea how much longer this train from Ohio would take to reach his hometown of Penn Hills, Pa.

The flames appeared before his eyes each time he tried to sleep. They were accompanied by the sound of the screaming child who panicked and tried to hide in a bedroom closest. Wyatt found the youngster and carried her to safety while trying to avoid her flailing arms. In doing so, he left his partner behind, breaking one of the main rules of firefighting.

Wyatt didn't think much of it at the time. Duane Wright had far more experience than he did. Leaving Duane for just a few minutes, to reunite a girl with her family, seemed like an acceptable risk. Then the roof caved in. Wyatt raced back inside the burning home, and he frantically called out Duane's name, but the roar of the fire drowned out his voice.

A frantic search ensued. Wyatt pushed a scorching beam aside as other members of his squad rushed to help him. The smoke was so thick that they could only see a few inches ahead. Wyatt pawed at the floor, desperately trying to find his friend. He bumped into something, and it took him a moment to realize that it was Duane's right leg.

Wyatt instinctively lifted the fallen firefighter and carried him outside until they reached a safe distance from the inferno. He gently lowered Duane onto an ambulance gurney and watched two EMTs try to revive the unconscious man. Despite their best efforts, they were unable to save his life.

Duane's funeral brought firefighters from all over Ohio and Pennsylvania, as men and women paid their respects to their fallen colleague. The governor of Ohio and his wife were among the attendees. A bishop from Duane's hometown of Pittsburgh presided over the funeral mass. A mile-long procession to the church closed streets all over Cleveland.

Wyatt wiped his eyes and sat back in his shaking seat. A woman sitting next to him read a spy novel. She never lifted her head as she concentrated on the book. Wyatt wondered how she managed to read without getting motion-sickness. He guessed it was a skill she developed over time.

Duane's service was just three weeks ago, and yet Wyatt found himself preparing to attend another funeral. He had answered his cell phone in the middle of the night when he recognized his brother Colin's number on the screen. Colin's voice shook as he spoke. Wyatt couldn't comprehend his brother's words at first. Soon it became clear. Their mother had lost her long battle with colon cancer. She died in her bed surrounded by her husband, David, a priest named Father Mills, and her younger son, Colin. However, her older son Wyatt was not there.

Wyatt rose and moved to the rear of the car. He stepped into the tiny bathroom. His trembling hands could barely work the knob of the sink. Wyatt turned it and cold water poured from the spout. He washed his face and hands and let the stinging water remain on his skin.

The short walk back to his seat was impeded by the shifting boxcar, and the gray-haired attendant pushing a drink cart. Wyatt's head pounded. "Do you have any ibuprofen?" he asked the attendant. He rubbed his temples to emphasize his pain.

The woman shook her head. "I'm sorry, we only have drinks and snacks," she said. She reached into the car and pulled out a miniature bag of pretzels. "Will these help?" she asked.

"I am afraid not," said Wyatt. "But thank you," he added. He slipped past the woman and her cart. The rocking train made it difficult for him to keep his balance. He banged into armrests as he fought to get back to his seat. He whispered apologies to the riders as he finally found his way. He sat down and closed his eyes.

The flames were around him again. The thick smoke blinded him. He began to breathe rapidly as his oxygen tank neared empty. Panic ran through him. He didn't know where he was, only that he was in danger. He pressed his palms against a wall, hoping to find his way outside. He kept telling himself that if he could just get outside, everything would be okay. He just couldn't find the exit.

Wyatt jolted himself awake. He rubbed his eyes again and saw a petite girl in a purple dress staring up at him. "Are you okay, mister?" she asked. Wyatt nodded. He guessed the girl was about 8-years-old. "You were tossing around in your chair," said the child. "Where you having a nightmare?"

Before Wyatt could answer, a woman in her late thirties grabbed the child by the arm. "Melissa," she said. "You shouldn't wander off like that." The woman lifted the girl into her arms and hugged her. "You don't want to bother the other passengers," said the mother. The woman glanced down at Wyatt. "I'm sorry," she said. "She is just a handful sometimes."

Wyatt smiled at the woman. "No problem," he said. He crossed his arms over his chest. "She is a lovely girl," he said. The woman nodded and walked away with the child still in her arms. Wyatt watched them disappear into the back of the train car.

Nervous energy quickly surged through Wyatt. He strummed his armrest with his fingers, while his feet tapped the floor. He felt blood pound in his head. He left Penn Hills five years ago and he was in no hurry to return. Wyatt loved his mother and he wished he had been there for her in the end, but the thought of returning home was too unbearable. Her death took away any chance of extending his self-imposed exile.

Wyatt pushed aside a window shade again as night overtook the area. He recognized a few lighted landmarks, and he knew he was close to home. He zipped up his black, leather coat and stuffed his hands into the pockets. His stomach churned again, but not from hunger. It was fear, plain and simple. For not too long from now, he would have to face his father.

The train finally stopped at the station as the noise of the brakes cut through the stale air. Passengers shuffled off the locomotive with bags in their hands. Wyatt picked up his two suitcases. He followed the others to the platform, and he looked around for his ride.

Wyatt put his suitcases down as Colin approached him. Colin wore his police deputy's uniform and he stood just a few inches shorter than Wyatt. Colin's blonde hair was neatly combed back, and his clothes were freshly pressed.

"It's good to see you, Wyatt," said Colin. He gave his older brother a quick and awkward hug. Wyatt hugged him back. "How long are you planning to stay?" asked Colin.

Wyatt shrugged. "I'm not really sure," he said. He rubbed his stubbled chin. "I took a leave of absence from work, so I don't have a set return date." He picked up the other suitcase and followed Colin toward the platform exit. "I'll just see how it goes."

They walked to the parking lot where Colin's police cruiser was parked. Wyatt stopped and glanced at the vehicle. "Is it alright that you're picking me up like this?" he asked. He nodded toward the cruiser. "You won't get in trouble, will you?"

Colin smiled and unlocked the car. "Relax," he said. "One of the perks of the job." He moved around the back of the vehicle until he stood next to Wyatt again. Colin opened one of the back doors. He put the suitcases into the rear of the cruiser. Colin shut the door. "C'mon, we gotta go. Dad is waiting for us."

Wyatt got in on the passenger side. Colin slid into the drivers' seat and started the engine. It purred to life as Colin pulled out of the parking spot. They left the parking lot and sped along Ben Franklin Road toward home. "Dad will be glad to see you," said Colin.

Wyatt looked out the window. "Are you sure?" he asked.

Colin nodded and kept his eyes on the road. "I'm sure," he said. "He may be gruff with you when we get home, but I know he misses you." He glanced at his brother. "And so do I." He lightly tapped Wyatt's left shoulder.

"I'd like to say that it's good to be home, but . . ." Wyatt's voice trailed off.

"Just be cool with Dad, and everything will be alright," said Colin. He turned the car onto Jefferson Street. "He is getting old, and he knows it. He wants to spend his Golden Years with his entire family, including you." Colin stopped the car at a red light.

"You look so grown up," said Wyatt. He lightly punched his brother's right shoulder. "When I left, you were still trying to find yourself. It looks like you succeeded." The light changed and Colin moved the car forward. "Dad must be proud of you," said Wyatt.

Colin rubbed his eyes. "You know how that goes," he said. "The old man is not good with words." The lawman grimaced.

Wyatt nodded and turned away from his brother. He looked out the window again as his hometown unfolded before him. He smiled when he saw the barber shop where he got his first haircut. The arcade on 5th Street was still there, and it was packed with kids and teens. The library, the police station, and the ice cream shop were just as he remembered them. Wyatt laughed at how little this sleepy town had changed.

Colin pulled the cruiser into a parking spot in front of *Harold's*, the sole diner in town and the hub of Penn Hills' social scene. "I could use a bite before we get home," said Colin. Wyatt nodded in agreement.

Wyatt got out of the car and breathed deeply. He caught the scent of *Harold's* famous meatloaf and mashed-potatoes special, the eatery's most popular dish. For the first time in weeks, Wyatt was hungry. He reached into his pocket and realized that he didn't have much money.

Wyatt awkwardly turned toward Colin. "I ah, don't have a lot on me," he stammered.

Colin laughed. "Don't worry, this one is on me," he said. He opened the door and held it open for his brother. Colin put a hand on Wyatt's right shoulder and followed him inside.

Wyatt smiled at the hostess. "Hello, Charlene," he said. "It's been a while."

Charlene's pretty face lit up. "Wyatt James!" she yelled. She flung herself at him and wrapped her arms around his shoulders. Most the patrons watched with amusement. "How are you?" she asked, after she pulled away from him. "You look terrific!"

Wyatt grinned. "You do too," he replied.

Charlene glanced at Colin before looking back at Wyatt. "A table for two, I see," she added. The men nodded. "Well, right this way," she said to them. Charlene put an arm around Wyatt as she led the men to their table.

The brothers sat down as Charlene handed them menus. "I recommend the broiled salmon with butter sauce, that's really good," she said. "And, of course, our meatloaf special. Tonight, it comes with corn, broccoli and mac-and-cheese." She opened her small notebook. "What can I get you guys to drink?" she asked.

"Coffee for me," said Wyatt. He opened the menu and read it like a child holding a favorite book. He quickly scanned the selections. They all looked good to him.

"I'll have some coffee, too," said Colin. "And can I also get a grilled-cheese sandwich with bacon?" he asked. "And some curly fries." He smiled at Charlene as she jotted down his order. She smiled back before refocusing on Wyatt.

"And what can I get you, Honey?" she asked. She softly tapped her pad with her pen.

Wyatt closed the menu. "I can't resist. Please bring me an order of meatloaf and mashed potatoes," he said. "With gravy on both." He rubbed his hands together before handing Charlene his menu. Colin handed his over too.

"I'll put them in right now," said Charlene. She turned and rushed to the order window. She pinned her order sheet to a spinning wheel, and she glanced back at the brothers. Wyatt thought he saw her stare at Colin, but he wasn't sure. He let out a small laugh.

"What's so funny?" asked Colin. He folded his hands and rested them on the table. A small smile formed. He instinctively glanced around the room before looking back at Wyatt.

Wyatt shook his head. "Nothing, really," he said. "I was just thinking how little this town has changed since I left. Even Charlene still seems the same." He tapped the edge of his menu. "It's like this is the town that time forgot."

"I wouldn't say that," said Colin. He sat back and chewed is bottom lip. "We have new, state-of-the-art computers and technology at the police station to help us fight crime." He pointed toward the fire station across the street. "Those guys have new trucks and equipment that arrived last summer. They are short-handed, but they do the best they can."

Wyatt nodded. "And yet Charlene is still slinging meatloaf here," said Wyatt. He paused and tilted his head. "Wait, what crime do you need high-tech to fight?" he asked. "Are jaywalkers getting sophisticated?"

Colin's face reddened. "We have our fair share of break-ins and car thefts to deal with," he said. He moved uncomfortably in his chair as Charlene brought Colin his coffee. He paused until she left. "The high-school delinquents keep us plenty busy."

Wyatt cleared his throat. "I'm sorry," he said. "I wasn't trying to minimize your work," he said. "But you have to admit, this is one sleepy town."

Colin sipped his coffee. "People here prefer it that way, and my fellow officers and I get paid to keep it that way." He drank more of the hot liquid. "I'd say we do a very good job."

"I'm sure you do," agreed Wyatt. He watched two women enter the eatery and sit down at the coffee bar. Wyatt leaned in and whispered to Colin. "Hey, aren't they the Landford sisters?" he asked.

Colin glanced over his shoulder before turning back to Wyatt. "Yes, they are," he said. "Susan and Michelle. Susan is a teacher, and Michelle is a loan officer at a bank." He sipped more coffee. Colin squinted. "Didn't you date Susan in high school?" he asked.

Wyatt laughed. "Yeah, for about a month. She was a real talker, that one." His smiled widened. "And a great kisser." He peeked around his brother and glanced at the women again. "Are either of them married?" he asked.

"No, they are both single," replied Colin. "But MicHelle is dating a contractor."

"And Susan?" asked Wyatt.

Colin shook his head. "As far as I know, she is not dating anyone." He turned and took a longer look at the ladies. He faced Wyatt. "Do you want to go over and say Hello to them?"

Wyatt shook his head. "No, I just ordered. I don't want to eat in front of them." He lightly strummed his fingers on the table. "Maybe another time."

Charlene arrived at the brothers' table with their food. Colin and Wyatt thanked her before digging into their meals. Wyatt wiped some gravy from his mouth with a napkin as he watched the Landford sisters finish their drinks and leave. He quietly ate his food as he remembered the short time he spent with Susan. It was so long ago that he wondered if she would even consider getting together again. He wondered if it would even be appropriate since he didn't know how long he was staying in town.

The brothers finished their meal, and Wyatt watched Colin pay the bill at the cashier stand. Charlene tried to flirt with Colin, but he was in too much of a hurry to notice her. Wyatt flashed Charlene a sympathetic smile, but she rolled her eyes at him. Wyatt followed Colin to the squad car.

Wyatt's hands shook as Colin pulled the vehicle onto the paved driveway of their childhood home. Colin got out of the vehicle, but Wyatt sat still for a moment. "Are you coming in?" asked Colin. Wyatt took a deep breath and slowed exited the cruiser.

"I'll get your suitcases," said Colin. He made a move toward the rear of the vehicle.

Wyatt waved his right hand at Colin. "Hold on," he said. Colin stopped and looked at his older brother. "Let's see how it goes first," said Wyatt. "No use carrying them in if we have to carry them back out again."

"I wouldn't worry about it," said Colin. He strode up beside his brother. "He is not going to make you leave. Just relax and try not to annoy him." He popped Wyatt on the shoulder. "I know that's asking a lot of you."

Wyatt walked a pace behind Colin. They reached the front door of the house and Colin used his key to open it. "Dad, we're here!" shouted Colin. He shut the door after Wyatt entered. They stood quietly still for a moment. Colin shrugged.

"Maybe he's not home," said Wyatt. He relaxed a little.

Colin shook his head. "I hear the TV in the den," he said. "Dad would never leave without turning it off." He glanced at Wyatt and spoke in a husky voice. "We don't own stock in the electric company, you know," he said, mocking their father.

The brothers laughed and continued down a hallway through the home. They passed the living room and the staircase to the second floor before walking through the kitchen to the den. They paused at the entrance to the back room. Colin put a hand up as they took a moment to compose themselves.

Wyatt saw their father sleeping on a couch. A 55-inch television across from it flashed images of a golf match. Two comfy chairs and a second couch filled out the room. A fireplace was tucked into a far corner. Pictures of the James family hung on the walls, along with paintings of lighthouses and fire stations.

Colin picked up a remote control and he turned off the television. He gently jostled his father's right shoulder. The old man slowly opened his eyes and wiped his mouth with a shirt sleeve. He nodded at Colin before noticing Wyatt.

"Well, look who it is," said David James. He made no attempt to stand up. "To what do we owe the honor of your presence?" he said.

"Dad, don't start," said Colin. "We just walked in the door."

David grimaced. "I'm surprised Wyatt knew how to find his way here," he snapped.

Wyatt slowly nodded. "It's great to see you too, Dad," he said. He wandered around the room, looking at the family photographs. He stopped in front of a picture of his mother. He picked it up and held it close to his face. "I'm sorry I didn't get to see her again before she passed," he said. He gently put the picture back in its place.

"Well, you had plenty of chances," said David. The brittle man gruffly rose to his feet. His legs shook as he walked toward Wyatt. Colin tried to intercept his father, but Wyatt waved him off. "You broke her heart," said David, as he came to a stop. "Not that you would care."

Wyatt took a step toward his father, and he stood just a few inches away from him. "I wanted to be here," said Wyatt. He glanced down at his feet. "It just got . . . complicated."

"Rubbish!" said David. "There is nothing complicated about taking a trip home," he said. He put his hands on his hips. "You buy a ticket, and you get on a train. It's not like you lived on the other side of the country." He paused and glared at his son. "If you wanted it bad enough, you would have been here."

"I think he gets the point, Dad," said Colin. The lawman stepped between his father and brother. He wrapped an arm around David and led him back to his chair. "Wyatt feels bad about what happened, and I think we owe it to him to forgive him," he said.

Wyatt watched Colin help their dad back into his seat. The old man kept his eyes on Wyatt, and the anger in his brown eyes was obvious. Colin spread a blanket out over David's lap. Without looking down, David pulled the blanket up to his chest.

"There, Dad," said Colin. "You rest and I will make your dinner." He motioned toward Wyatt with his head. "We will be back soon," said Colin. He picked up the remote and turned the television back on.

Once they made it into the hallway, Wyatt stopped and put a hand on Colin's right shoulder. "Thanks," said Wyatt. "For having my back in there." He wanted to say more, but nothing intelligent came to him.

Colin turned and led the way back to the kitchen. He removed a frying pan from a cabinet and placed it on the stove. Wyatt sat in a kitchen chair, and he watched his brother prepare food for David. "I wasn't lying," said Wyatt. "I really did want to be here before."

"You don't have to convince me," said Colin. He grabbed a container of hamburger meat, and a few bags of vegetables from the refrigerator. Colin placed them on the kitchen counter, and he started slicing the vegetables. "I know how hectic life can be."

"Dad's right," said Wyatt. He rested his hands in his lap. "I should have found a way to get back here sooner." He slowly shook his head. "I don't really blame him for being mad at me." He sighed. "I guess I would be too, if I were him."

Colin put the knife down. "Then let this be a new beginning," said Colin. "Spend as much time with Dad as you can. He will complain about it at first, but he'll soon appreciate what you are doing. Trust me, deep down he is elated that you are home."

"That's hard to believe," said Wyatt. Colin frowned at him. "Alright, alright, I will give it a try," said Wyatt. Colin went back to his chore. Wyatt laughed. "When did you become the happy homemaker?" he asked.

Colin shrugged. "It just kind of happened," he said. "Necessity, I guess."

Wyatt leaned back in his chair. He watched in amazement as Colin prepared the meal like a gourmet chef. *I guess some things have changed around here*, thought Wyatt. He rested his chin on the tops of hands. *So now it's my turn.*

Chapter Two

The flames felt like they were burning through Wyatt's gear. He stumbled through the thick smoke with Duane Wright behind him. A little girl was somewhere in this inferno and the firefighters were determined to save her. Wyatt called out the little girl's name as he carefully moved debris that was blocking his path.

Wyatt felt like they were moving in circles and not making any progress. He saw the same painting of a boat on a lake three times as it melted on a wall. Wyatt turned back to check on Duane, but he couldn't see more than a few feet around him. "Are you still with me?" he shouted to his partner.

"Yeah, I'm here," responded Duane. "Keep going. This roof won't last much longer."

Wyatt faced forward and continued his meticulous search. The floorboards crunched under his feet. He could feel them starting to give out. He tried to slow his breathing to conserve his oxygen and to keep himself calm. The smell of burning plastic made his eyes water.

He came upon a closed closet door. Wyatt slowly opened it and saw a small child huddled up against the wall. He quickly reached in and swooped the child into his arms. She began to panic, and her arms flailed about. "It's alright, sweetheart," he said to her. "I got you. I'm going to take you to your family."

Wyatt turned and nearly bumped into Duane. "I found her," he said.

Duane nodded and stepped aside. Wyatt marched past his partner, expecting Duane to immediately follow him. It wasn't until Wyatt was outside with the girl in his arms that he noticed Duane's absence. He handed the girl to EMTs and rushed back inside the burning home.

Three other firefighters helped Wyatt search for Duane. They pushed aside burned up furniture and other debris. Wyatt called out Duane's name, but he didn't get a response. The house jolted as if an earthquake had hit. Wyatt knew his squad was running out of time.

Wyatt felt around the floor with his hands. He touched something that moved. Wyatt wiped the fog from his facemask and pointed his flashlight at the floor. He saw an enormous shoe on the body of a fallen man. He reached down and saw Duane's closed eyes through his friend's helmet.

"I've got him!" Wyatt shouted to his squad. He picked up his friend and carried him over his shoulder. He watched in horror as Duane's lower body slammed to the ground. "What the Hell?" he shouted.

Duane's upper body remained in Wyatt's arms. Confused, he tried to grab the lower body, only to drop what was in his hands. Wyatt froze, unable to process what he was seeing. It looked like Duane's body were cut in two. "I need help over here!" he shouted.

Wyatt dropped to his knees and tried to lift all of Duane's body. No matter what he did, he could not get a strong grip on either section. He yelled for help again, but no one came to assist him. He kept trying to save his friend, and he kept failing.

Wyatt sat up in bed with his entire body shaking. The room was pitch black, except for the light from an electronic clock. He wiped his sweaty face as his heart pounded. Wyatt had not gotten used to the nightmares. They kept nipping at his mind like a hungry dog. He took several deep breaths before getting out of bed and putting on a sweatshirt, a pair of jeans, and his sneakers.

It was still dark outside when Wyatt closed the front door behind him. He rubbed his cold hands together before stuffing them into his coat pockets. His breath hung around his face. Wyatt walked unsteadily along the sidewalk as his family home disappeared into the darkness. He carefully crossed street corners as the images of the fire that killed Duane filled his mind.

Despite the chilly air and a lingering pain in his legs, Wyatt hiked for miles until he found himself on the edge of Ben Franklin Road. The town was deserted, save for a lone truck dropping off bundles of morning newspapers. Wyatt passed the gas station and the mini-mart. He was about to cross over Adams Boulevard when he stopped and looked in the window of *Smiley's Café*.

He slowly entered the eatery and drifted toward the coffee bar. There he found Susan Landford sipping coffee and reading from her cell phone. "Excuse me, is this seat taken?" he asked Susan. She grunted without looking up. "Thank you," he replied.

The barista asked Wyatt what he wanted. Wyatt glanced at Susan with a smile. "I would like a chocolate mocha with marshmallows, sprinkles, and a hint of honey," he said. The barista raised her eyebrows as she turned to make the order.

Susan lifted her eyes and stared at Wyatt. A smile formed on her face. "There is only one person I know weird enough to order that drink," she said. She rose and moved toward Wyatt. "Oh my god, it's you!" she said. She wrapped her arms around him as he rose from his seat. "How long has it been?" she asked.

Wyatt allowed himself to linger in her arms for a moment. "Too long," he said. He eased back onto his stool as Susan sat down again. "You look amazing," said Wyatt.

"Thank you," replied Susan. She quickly brushed his right shoulder with her hand. "You look . . . very fit." she added. She let out a nervous laugh. "Do you work out a lot?" she asked.

Wyatt shrugged. "I little, sometimes," he said. The barista handed him his coffee. He blew on it before sipping the hot liquid. "I'm a firefighter," he said. He paused and his face soured. "Well, I was one."

Susan rested her chin on her hands. "You were one?" she asked. Wyatt nodded. "What happened?" she asked. She picked up her cup and wrapped her fingers around it before sipping the coffee. The steam rose over her face.

Wyatt looked down at the counter for a moment. "I had a bad experience," he said. He peered up at Susan. "Now I'm not sure what I am." He turned his head and sighed. Wyatt rubbed his chin as he turned back to face Susan.

Susan gently lowered her right hand onto Wyatt's wrist. "I was sorry to hear about your mother," she said. "She was a wonderful woman." She withdrew her hand. "I worked with her every year at the summer carnival. Everyone in town loved her."

"Thank you," said Wyatt. He crossed his arms over his chest. "I tried to get back here before, but my schedule was too hectic," he said. He pressed his lips together. "I should have tried harder."

Susan tilted her head and lightly tapped her fingers against the cup in her hands. "Your mother loved you very much. She talked about you and Colin all the time. She was very proud of her sons." Susan put on a smile. "I can see why. Both of you are good men."

"Colin is a great guy," said Wyatt. "I'm glad he was here for her." He looked around the nearly empty café before his eyes settled on Susan. "Do you normally get coffee this early in the morning?" he asked.

Susan put her cup down on the counter. "No. I'm usually just getting up right about now. But today we have conferences with the parents. They make me extremely nervous." She nodded to emphasize the point. "I couldn't sleep."

"Oh, so you are a schoolteacher?" asked Wyatt. Susan nodded. "What grade level?"

"Seventh and eighth," said Susan. She picked up a napkin and wrang it in her hands. "I like them better than high school kids. Mine are well-behaved and they don't have that false sense of importance that most older kids have."

Wyatt laughed. "Yeah, I was a bit of a Hellraiser when I was in high school," he said. "I remember always wanting to have fun, and to not listen to my parents. It drove them crazy. Especially my father." He paused and took a deep breath. "Colin was the sensible one. Always had good grades. He ran track and he played basketball."

"I remember," said Susan. "I was a cheerleader for four years. Colin was great at basketball, but it seemed like his heart wasn't in it." She finished her coffee, and she pushed the empty cup away from her. "Are we going to ignore the elephant in the room or are you going to ask me out?" she asked.

Wyatt smiled. “Wow! You are bold. I remember that about you.”

Susan leaned toward Wyatt and whispered. “You know what I remember about you?” she asked. Wyatt shrugged. “That you were a great kisser,” she said.

They breathlessly stared at each other, but neither one made the next move.

“Can I get you anything else?” asked the barista. She stood chomping gum in her mouth as the tense moment ended. Susan leaned back in her seat. Wyatt rubbed the back of his neck and glared at the intruder. “I guess not,” said the barista. She quicky wrote two bills and laid them on the counter. She rushed off without looking back.

Susan pulled out her cell phone and glanced down at it. “Well, it’s getting late,” she said. She took a few dollars out of her pocket and dropped them on the counter. “I need to get ready for work.” She reached out and touched Wyatt’s right arm. “It really was great seeing you again. We should get together one night.”

Wyatt smiled. “I would like that.” He watched Susan gather her belongings and strut toward the exit. He took out his wallet and tossed a few dollars onto the counter. Wyatt exited the café and continued his trek through town.

The wind blew through the area, chilling Wyatt to his bones. Some local folks greeted him as his sight-seeing tour continued. There were smiles, hugs, and questions from those he encountered. Despite his aimlessness and growing sense of dread, part of him was glad he was walking these familiar streets again. It was a bit therapeutic.

Wyatt passed a drug store when a police car flew by him with its lights flashing and its siren blaring. He stopped dead in his tracks and watched the vehicle turn left at the next intersection. Soon, other police cars, fire trucks, and EMT vehicles roared down the road in the same direction. Wyatt hurried along the sidewalk to see where they were going.

Smoke rose from a church that was engulfed in flames. Firefighters positioned themselves strategically, with hoses pouring water on the building. The police cars blocked off the area as residents lined up to see what was happening. A news crew sprung from a van and started filming the incident.

Wyatt fought the urge to jump in and help. Instead, he moved slowly through the crowd until he found the local fire chief standing with two firefighters. Wyatt recognized the officer. Chief Sam Carpenter pointed toward the front of the church. “We need to concentrate more on the entrance!” he shouted. One of the firefighters ran off and relayed that message to his colleagues. “Where is that truck from Morrisville?” asked the chief.

“They’re on their way,” said the other firefighter. Wyatt was surprised to hear a woman’s voice. “They hit traffic on Johnson Avenue.” The firefighter turned toward the crowd and Wyatt saw her face. He thought she looked familiar, but he wasn’t sure. “We’ve got to keep these people back,” she said.

Wyatt watched the female firefighter turn to a nearby police officer. “The crowd is too close,” she said. “Please get them back.” The police officer nodded and ordered the spectators to back up. The firefighter darted toward the church and helped another maneuver a firehose.

The Morrisville fire truck arrived. Wyatt watched the firefighters descend the vehicle and join the battle. The driver approached Chief Carpenter and the men shook hands. “Sorry sir,” said the driver. “We got here as fast as we could.”

"I appreciate that," said Carpenter. "It's nearly under control, but I'm worried about this wind. That repair shop next door is filled with chemicals." The chief pointed toward the adjoining auto repair facility. "If the fire spreads to it, we will be in real trouble. Have your men focus on the flames on that side of the church."

The driver nodded and rushed toward his crew. They quickly set up and aimed their hoses at the far end of the church. The strategy worked, and the fire was contained to the church. A half-hour later, the fire was completely out.

Most of the spectators dispersed, but Wyatt stayed and watched the crews wrap up their work. He saw the female firefighter standing with Carpenter. She drank water from a plastic bottle as Carpenter spoke to her. Wyatt moved forward to listen to what they were saying.

"You think this was deliberately set?" asked Carpenter. The woman nodded. The chief rubbed his neck. "We haven't had an arson here in years. We'll need to contact the county arson inspector's office." He took out his cell phone and dialed a number.

The woman turned and she caught Wyatt's eyes. "Can I help you, sir?" she asked.

Wyatt shook his head. He glanced at the front of her jacket and saw K. Carpenter stitched on the left shoulder. "What makes you think this was arson?" he asked. He slowly moved his hands into his coat pockets as the wind kicked up again.

The woman took a step toward him. "Are you a reporter?" she asked.

"No," said Wyatt. "I'm a firefighter," he said. He removed his wallet and showed her his ID. "I'm Wyatt James," he said. "I grew up here." He put his wallet back in his pocket.

The woman nodded. "I'm Kasey Carpenter." They shook hands. "I know your brother, Colin," she added. "We went to school together."

Wyatt smiled. *That's why she looked familiar*, he thought. "How did this fire start?"

Kasey leaned toward Wyatt. "We found empty kerosene containers behind the church," she said. "Whoever did this just left them there. The cops are dusting for prints." She turned to face the captain. "Dad, what did they say?" she asked him.

Carpenter put his cell phone in his pocket, and he stepped toward Wyatt and Kasey. "Who is this?" he asked, pointing at Wyatt. Kasey introduced the men to each other. "Wyatt James?" asked Carpenter. "Your brother is Colin James?"

"Yes, sir," replied Wyatt. "He is."

"He is a good police officer," said Carpenter. "Too bad he didn't follow in your dad's footsteps. We need all the good men we can get in the fire department." He turned in the direction of the church. "Who the Hell would burn down a church?" he asked.

Wyatt shrugged. "Could be a bunch of rebellious teens," he suggested. "Maybe they came out here to drink and things got out of hand." He glanced at Carpenter and saw that the chief didn't look impressed with his theory. "Or not."

Carpenter shook his head. "No, a bunch of drunken teens wouldn't use kerosene. Gas is much cheaper and easier to get." The captain grimaced. "There was much more planning involved here." He stepped away and spoke to the driver of the visiting squad.

"I need to get going too," said Kasey. She put out her right hand and Wyatt shook it. "Hey, if you ever want to work here, let me know. We could always use the help." Kasey let go of his hand and spun around. She rushed over to her firetruck and helped the others load it.

****

Wyatt fixed the knot of his tie as he stared at his reflection in the mirror. His hands shook. He closed his eyes and tried to settle down. He promised himself that he would try to keep it together during the service. His eyes slowly opened as Colin appeared in the mirror.

Wyatt quickly inhaled. He put his right hand on his chest. "You startled me," he said. He finished fussing with his tie and turned to face his brother. He lightly brushed some lint from Colin's right shoulder. "You look great, Colin," he said. Wyatt shook his head. "You look better than I do."

"It's not a competition," said Colin. He rested a hand on Wyatt's right shoulder. "Are you ready?" he asked. "It's nearly time to go."

Wyatt stood frozen for a moment. "I hate funerals," he said. Colin raised his eyebrows. "I know, everyone does. But in our line of work, we go to too many of them." Wyatt drifted toward his closet, and he took out his suit jacket. He put it on and turned to see his reflection again.

"You could be on the cover of GQ," said Colin. He lightly tapped his brother's back. "Stop admiring yourself, and let's get downstairs. There are a few people here to see you, and we need to get to the service on time."

The brothers descended the staircase and walked into the living room. Wyatt saw parishioners from his mother's church as they milled around. David James sat on a couch with a beer in his hand. Wyatt shook his head in embarrassment as the old man looked like a miserable child at a school function.

The James brothers mingled with the visitors. They shook hands, accepted hugs, and tried to make their guests feel comfortable. Wyatt peeked over at their father, as the old man sat stoically on the couch. David stared forward without speaking to anyone.

The pastor said all the right words from the Bible as mourners wept at the graveside of Ethel James. Wyatt stood next to Colin, while David kept his head down as he stood beside his younger son. It was a cloudy, chilly morning and Wyatt was glad that the rain waited until the service was over. Everyone dashed to their vehicles as the first drops began to fall.

Colin arranged the reception at the James' home. A local caterer provided lunch-time fare, with meatball subs, tuna salad, ham and cheese sandwiches, wine, soda, and various cakes and cookies. Nearly everyone from the funeral attended the crowded event in the living room. The somber tone occasionally lightened as mourners recalled their favorite memories of Ethel James.

Wyatt was exhausted. More nightmares about Duane's death kept him from getting decent sleep. He rubbed his tired eyes as he sat in a chair and observed the event. He started to nod off when he felt a hand on his right shoulder. His eyes snapped open.

"It's rude to sleep in front of all these guests," said Susan Landford. She sat down in an empty chair beside Wyatt. "Here, this should help." She handed him a cup of steaming coffee. "I'm sorry, but I wasn't able to find any marshmallows, sprinkles, or honey."

Wyatt laughed. "Thanks, this will do." He sipped the coffee and tried to breathe in the stuffy room. "Thank you for coming. It means a lot to me." He reached over and gently squeezed her left hand.

"I wouldn't miss this for the world," said Susan. She sipped coffee from her own cup. "I really liked your mother. She had a way of making people feel better, just by talking with them. She'll be greatly missed."

"Yes, she will," said Wyatt. He looked around the room. "I knew she had a lot of friends, but I didn't expect this many people to be here. Mom would have been proud." He drank more coffee and felt his head start to clear.

"How long are you staying in town?" asked Susan. She finished her drink and put the cup on an end table. Susan folded her slim fingers and rested her hands in her lap.

Wyatt noticed the way the light glittered off her short, brown hair that hung just above her shoulders. Despite his grief, he couldn't help feeling attracted to Susan. The years had only made her more beautiful. Wyatt fought off the urge to kiss her.

"I don't know," said Wyatt. He swallowed hard. "I still have my job in Ohio, but I might not go back." He shrugged. "I guess it depends on how much I'm needed here."

Susan smiled. "For what it's worth, I hope you stay here," she said.

Wyatt looked into her eyes and his passion burned hotter. He felt his chest tighten, and his throat dry up. "I'm glad you feel that way," he said.

"Excuse me," said someone who had approached from Wyatt's right side. Wyatt cleared his throat and turned to see Chief Carpenter's daughter standing before him. Wyatt rose to his feet to greet her. "I'm sorry to interrupt," said Kasey Carpenter. "I just wanted to offer my condolences," she said.

"Thank you," replied Wyatt. Susan stood up beside Wyatt as he shook Kasey's hand. He turned toward Susan. "Susan, this is Kasey Carpenter." Wyatt looked back at the firefighter. "Kasey, this is Susan Landford."

"Yes, we've met," said Susan. She slowly wrapped her right arm around Wyatt.

"This might not be the best time," said Kasey. "But I wanted to let you know that the police didn't find any fingerprints on those kerosene containers we found behind the church. Whoever set that fire must have been wearing gloves."

Wyatt watched his brother approach them. "Are we talking shop?" asked Colin.

Kasey's face reddened. "I'm sorry," she said. "I just thought Wyatt would want to know."

"No problem," said Colin. He looked at Susan. "Susan, you look wonderful. Thank you for coming today." Susan nodded at Colin. The police officer turned to Kasey. "You are a vision, as always." Kasey blushed. "But maybe we should talk about this later. I'm sure you understand."

"Yes," said Kasey. "Again, I'm sorry."

Colin took Kasey by her right arm. "Kasey, have you had the chance to try these oatmeal cookies?" he asked. "They are the best in town." Colin guided Kasey away from Wyatt and Susan.

"Your brother could always read a room," said Susan.

Wyatt nodded. "Yes, he is a smoothie."

Susan turned to face Wyatt. “What are you doing for dinner tomorrow night?” she asked.

Wyatt smiled. “I’m taking you to the best restaurant in town,” he said. “One without golden arches in front.”

“That sounds lovely,” said Susan.

Chapter Three

The grease sizzled in the pan. Kasey Carpenter cautiously turned the bacon strips with a fork. She beat a large bowl of eggs and poured them into a skillet. Kasey lowered sausage patties into another pan, and she leaned back as a wave of boiling steam rose toward her. She turned up the speed of the ceiling fan to keep the smoke detectors from going off. The last thing she needed to do was start a fire at a firehouse.

Her coworkers at Penn Hills Station One sat in the den watching television. Their chatter traveled all the way into the kitchen. Kasey smiled as she worked. She liked it when her fellow firefighters had a good time. The job was tense enough without internal fighting, and the pressure of always being ready to respond to an alarm took its toll on most people in her profession.

Kasey transferred the cooked food to several plates as Lance Davis entered and approached her. "Everything smells great in here," he said. He moved a little too close to Kasey, and she inched away from him. Lance picked up a piece of bacon and chomped down on it. "You are a great cook," he said. He finished the slice. "You're wasting your talents here. You should be a chef," he said.

"No thanks," replied Kasey. "I don't mind doing this every now and then, but I'd hate to have to do it fulltime." She put a pan into the sink. "Besides, without me, you guys would starve." She tried to inch her way around Lance, but she bumped into him instead.

Kasey stopped in her tracks. She waved her hands at Lance. "Will you please back up?" she asked. Lance remained in place and stared at her. "Lance, really! Back up!"

The lean firefighter slowly eased backward, never taking his eyes off Kasey. “You look beautiful, Kasey,” he said. “More so every day.” His smile expanded. “I never get tired of seeing your face. And I never will.”

Kasey moved away from Lance, and she put two plates on the island in the middle of the kitchen. “Can you please get the rest?” she asked. She proceeded to take utensils out of a drawer from another cabinet. She placed a fork and knife beside each plate.

“Kasey, there is something I want to ask you,” said Lance, as he put two plates on the island. Kasey had her back to Lance, and she felt the panic rise in her. Lance moved toward her and gently took her hands. “We’ve been working together for 8 months now,” he said. “I’d like to think that we’ve built up a strong friendship. One based on honesty and respect.” He took a deep breath and continued. “Kasey, will you go out with me this weekend?” he asked.

The panic inside her escalated. She slowed her breathing. “Lance, you know I think you are a great guy, and a top-notch firefighter, but I can’t go out with you.” She paused to let that sink in. “We’ve been through this before. I don’t date firefighters.”

Lance’s smile faded. He gave a quick nod. “I know. You have told me that before. I was just hoping you had changed your mind.” He leaned against the island. “I was at Ethel James’ reception. I saw the way you looked at Wyatt James. He is a firefighter. Are you going to go out with him?” he asked.

“No,” replied Kasey. She frowned at Lance. “I barely know the guy,” she said. “All I know is that he has a reputation as a solid firefighter. I think the squad could use him.”

Lance stared at her until he realized what he was doing. “I’m sorry,” he said, turning away from Kasey. He took a few steps toward the door before turning around again. “I don’t want you to feel uncomfortable around me. I just want you to do how I feel about you." He shrugged. "Maybe someday you'll feel that way about me."

Kasey leaned against a counter and watched Lance exit the kitchen. She pressed her trembling lips together as she attempted to slow her breathing. *Why not?* she thought. *He is as good looking a guy as anyone else in this town. Maybe it is time to break the rules.* She closed her eyes and thought about a life as Mrs. Davis: Having kids, going food shopping, taking vacations, and lugging laundry baskets to the washer and dryer in their home.

Kasey snapped out of her daydream when Chief Carpenter entered the kitchen. He stopped in front of the plate of bacon, and he took a piece. "How are you this fine morning?" he asked his daughter.

The cook smiled at her dad. "I'm okay," she said. Kasey poured the captain a hot cup of coffee and handed it to him. "Here, drink this," she said. Kasey went to the refrigerator and removed a carton of orange juice. She filled a few glasses from a cabinet and left them on the island.

"I saw Lance leave just now," said Carpenter. Kasey nodded as she poured herself a new, hot coffee. "Are you two getting along?" asked the captain.

Kasey sipped her coffee. "Just peachy," she replied. She moved past her father and yelled to the other firefighters. "If you guys can tear yourselves away from the TV, breakfast is ready." The men got up as one of them turned off the TV with the remote.

Carpenter whispered to his daughter as the others grabbed plates of food. "I like Lance," he told her. "He's a good man, and I think he could be good for you." Carpenter kissed Kasey on the forehead. "Just think about it," he said.

Kasey made a plate for herself, and she sat down at the kitchen table across from Lance. The others joked with each other as they ate. Kasey found herself staring at Lance. When he looked up at her, she quickly looked away. *Great,* she thought. *I'm back in middle school.*

Chief Carpenter sipped some orange juice before he addressed his daughter. "Kasey, what is the latest on the church fire?" he asked. "Do the police have any leads yet?" He took another sip as his daughter gathered her thoughts.

"No leads yet," said Kasey. She wiped her mouth with a napkin. "Colin James told me that the police have a few suspects, but nothing official yet." She bit a slice of toasted bread and slowly chewed it.

"When was the last time you spoke to Colin?" asked Carpenter. He dug into his plate with gusto. He chewed his food as he waited for an answer.

"I called the police station this morning," replied Kasey. "I talked to Colin," she said. She took another sip of her drink. "He didn't sound hopeful."

Carpenter tilted his head. "I was afraid of that," he said. He finished his meal, and he addressed the team. "We should all be more vigilant. Next time they might go after one of us." He rubbed his reddened eyes. "No more leaving separately at night. Do so in pairs. And don't let any strangers get too close," he warned. "That's an order."

The crew acknowledged him in unison.

"Good," said Carpenter. "Now let's finish up and get back to work."

The men brought their empty plates and glasses into the kitchen and placed them in the sink. Kasey was the last to finish eating, and the kitchen was nearly empty when she carried in her plate and glass. She stood still for a moment, waiting for someone in her crew to clean up. "Hey, I cooked!" she yelled, as the firefighters walked toward the garage. "I'm not cleaning up," she said. Kasey slumped against a counter when she realized that she wasn't getting any help. "You guys suck!" she yelled.

****

Kasey sat in a camping chair and watched her crew members play basketball on the half-court behind the fire station. The four-on-four teams played a friendly game with little contact. Kasey laughed as the guys horsed around on the court. Though she tried to hide hit, she couldn't keep herself from staring at Lance.

Lance wore a white t-shirt and gray shorts. He glided around the court, easily sinking baskets with his natural abilities. He wiped sweat from his forehead and set up to guard his counterpart. Lance stole a soft pass and he rushed to the net and dunked the ball.

Kasey whistled and cheered as Lance set up again to play defense. He glanced at Kasey and flashed her a smile. Kasey swallowed and tried to act casually. Her eyelashes fluttered and she hid her clenched fists. Lance's team stopped their opponents again, before serving the ball to Lance. He shot from near the foul line and the ball zipped into the hoop.

The guys took a break and invited Kasey onto the court. She dribbled the ball with her right hand before expertly switching to her left hand. "Wow, that's impressive," said Lance. He edged closer to her. "Can you shoot?" he asked.

"She can shoot better than any of you morons," said Chief Carpenter, as he exited the station house and walked toward the court. "She played varsity basketball in high school, and she could have played college ball if she wanted to."

"I find that hard to believe," said one of the crewmen.

"Show them, honey," said the captain. He stood next to Lance.

Kasey dribbled the ball before firing a shot that hit the backboard and sunk softly into the net. She recovered the ball and took three more shots from different spots on the court. All of them went into the hoop.

"Anyone want to go one on one?" asked Kasey. She looked directly at Lance. "I might even spot you some points."

The guys hooted and hollered at her, but no one took her up on her offer.

Kasey took a step toward Lance. "You're not afraid, are you?" she asked. She passed the ball to Lance. He caught it with one hand and pulled it toward his right hip.

"Bring it on," he said. The guys hooted some more. Lance tossed the ball to Kasey. "You can bring it out."

Kasey dribbled the ball and slickly moved around Lance on her way to the basket. She scored on a layup as her opponent stood watching. Kasey flipped the ball to Lance. "You've got to do better than that to stop me," she said.

Lance nodded. He backed toward the net, guarding the ball with his body. Kasey tried to reach around him, but he shifted and moved from side to side. Lance planted his feet and shot toward the net. The ball found its target and slipped through the white fabric.

Kasey took the ball and rushed forward. She stopped suddenly and shot at the net as Lance tried to stop his momentum. The ball hit the rim and ricocheted back to her. Kasey rushed around Lance and scored another layup. She turned and smiled at Lance as the other guys cheered. "I can do this all day," she said.

The duel turned into a dance as both players touched each other as much as possible. The captain and the other crewmen gradually left Kasey and Lance alone to work out their sexual frustrations. Kasey's mind was so locked in on her opponent that she didn't realize that the others were gone. Not until she drove for another layup and Lance tackled her.

The players tumbled to the ground as the ball rolled off the court. Kasey landed on her back with Lance on top of her. She froze and tried to catch her breath. A sudden pain in her right shoulder made her wince. Lance noticed and he pushed himself to his feet. "Are you hurt?" he asked. He offered her a hand.

The pain in Kasey's shoulder quickly subsided. She took Lance's hand and he pulled her to her feet. "I think that was a foul," she said. She moved passed him and picked up the basketball. Kasey returned to the court and stood at the foul line. She took two shots and made them both. She tossed him the ball. "Shall we continue?" she asked.

Lance dribbled the ball twice as he shook his head. "No," he replied. "You won that one." He held the ball in his right arm. "But I'll want a rematch soon," he said. He lightly chucked the ball back to her.

"I don't know about rematch," said Kasey. She rolled the ball in her hands. "But our shift is over, and I am hungry. What you say we get some dinner?" she asked.

"Dinner?" asked Lance. "As in a date?"

"Dinner," replied Kasey. "As in two friends sharing a meal. Remember, I don't date firefighters." She winked at him. Lance nodded and walked toward her. "And since you lost," added Kasey, "you're buying."

****

The lasagna looked good on the menu, but Kasey found it sitting heavy in her stomach as the waiter asked the couple if they wanted dessert. "No, I'm good," said Kasey. She picked up her glass and drank some water. She took a shallow breath and let it out slowly.

"Just the check," said Lance. He smiled at the waiter. The man in the dark suit smiled back and returned to the front of the restaurant. Lance leaned back in his seat. "How was your meal?" he asked Kasey.

"It was delicious," she said. She tapped her flat stomach. "It will take a long walk to burn if off." She wiped her mouth with her crumpled napkin. "It's warm out. How about a walk on the pier? We can get some fresh air."

Lance smiled. "Sounds good to me," he said. The waiter returned and handed the bill to Lance, who slid his credit card inside the brown holder. The waiter nodded and left to charge the card. "There's a great ice cream shop on the pier. And this time, you're buying."

Kasey and Lance strolled along the crowded pier as the sun dropped below the horizon. They walked side-by-side but neither tried touch the other. A slight breeze blew through the crowd, giving some relief to the end of a hot day.

The friends stopped and leaned back against a railing. Kasey watched others walk by them. Some folks carried bags filled with purchases, while others just held hands. A little boy with chocolate sauce on his face and hands nearly bumped into Lance.

Kasey heard a boat horn behind her, so she turned to face the river. She saw several fishing boats among the vessels in the water. Kasey smiled. "My grandfather drove a boat when he was younger," she said. "He used to tell me all kinds of stories."

"He's lucky," said Lance. Kasey thought his face looked a little pale. "I don't do so well on the water," he admitted. "My stomach gets tied in knots." He glanced at Kasey, who was holding back a laugh. "Sure, you think it's funny, but nothing ever helped it. Not medication. Not those wrists bands. Nothing." Lance sighed. "It sucks because I'd have such a blast on a boat if it didn't make me want to throw up."

"That's too bad," replied Kasey. "I love boats. I love the still of the water, the sound of the engines, the feel of the sun beating down." She closed her eyes and leaned her head back. "I love boating on the ocean too," she added. "There you've got the crashing of the waves, and the sounds of the seabirds," she said. She reopened her eyes. "And let's not forget the sight of guys on the beach playing volleyball. Very sexy."

"The beach I can handle," said Lance. "As long as I stay on land." They turned around to face the shops again. Lance pointed to their left. "There's Morty's ice cream shop," he said. "Let's stop there for dessert," he suggested.

"Sounds good," said Kasey. She let Lance lead the way. They weaved through the crowd until they were in front of the ice cream shop. Kasey rubbed her hands in anticipation. She looked at the menu board and tried to decide what she wanted.

A man and a woman at the front of the line held hands and giggled as they gave their order. Kasey thought something seemed familiar about them. When the man turned around, Kasey's shoulders slumped. She diverted her eyes and tried to hide behind Lance.

"What's wrong?" asked Lance. He touched Kasey's right arm and seemed ready to catch her if she fell.

Kasey cleared her throat. "Can we skip this for now?" she asked. Lance nodded. "Great, come on," she said. She nearly pulled Lance out of his sneakers as they rushed away from the food stand. They stopped at the railing and Kasey looked over at the other couple. Wyatt James and Susan Landford continued laughing as they ate their ice cream cones. Neither seemed to notice Kasey or her quick retreat.

"Are you alright?" asked Lance. He lowered his eyebrows. "You are acting weird."

Kasey finally looked over at him. "I'm feeling a bit tired," she said. "Can you please take me home?" she asked.

"Yeah, sure," said Lance. He seemed confused. "If that's what you want."

"It is," said Kasey. She lightly punched Lance on the right shoulder.

Lance shook his head as he followed Kasey back to his vehicle.

Chapter Four

Kasey Carpenter entered the crowded room and smiled at the impeccably dressed men and women. Some sat at tables covered in white cloths with fine dishes and glasses, while other patrons danced on the hardwood floor under the spinning globe. Kasey passed a full-length mirror and saw that she was wearing a stunning red dress with black shoes. She had no idea where she was, but that didn't stop her from wanting to dance.

She found her way to the dance floor despite not having a partner. She spun around like a child and reached for the dizzying globe above her. The crowd on the dance floor parted, and Kasey saw Lance moving toward her. He wore a smooth, black tuxedo and his hair was neatly combed back. He reached Kasey and took her by the hands. Without a word, they danced to the thundering music until Lance pulled her close to him.

"You look beautiful, my dear," he said to her. He lightly touched her chin. "I've never seen you more radiant." He nuzzled his chin on her left shoulder and pulled her into his arms. "I wish this night would never end."

Kasey was too caught up in the moment to question what was happening. She decided just to go with it. She felt safe in Lance's arms. His body heat warmed her, and their feet moved in unison with the music.

Lance kissed her passionately as confetti fell from the ceiling. Kasey wondered if it were New Year's Eve, and she just forgot the date. She didn't care. She was flying high and nothing else mattered. Their kisses became more heated as they breathlessly danced together.

The music changed and Kasey suddenly had trouble with her sight. Everything became blurry and dark. She felt Lance's body slip away from hers. She reached out for him, but he was no longer there. Something compelled her to turn around. When she did, she saw a stranger reaching out for her.

The stranger stepped closer, and Kasey finally recognized him. It was Wyatt James. Behind him stood Susan Landford, but she swiftly disappeared. Wyatt took Kasey by the shoulders and gently guided her to an open spot on the dance floor. "Dance with me," he said. "I am the one you are supposed to be with," he said.

Kasey and Wyatt glided across the dance floor. He stared into her eyes as they maneuvered to the music. Wyatt pressed his cheek against hers. "No one dances as wonderfully as you do," he said. He kissed her lips before gently pulling away. "I want to spend the rest of my life with you."

The music stopped and everyone turned to look at Kasey. Chief Carpenter rushed toward her dressed in his firefighting uniform. "Hurry!" he shouted. "There's a fire at the grammar school. We need to go now!"

Kasey turned toward Wyatt. "I can't go with you," he said. "I don't do that anymore."

Lance appeared with his gear on. "Come on!" he shouted. "There's no time!"

Kasey's mind froze. She couldn't decide what to do. She looked down and discovered that her gorgeous red dress was gone. She now wore her fire-fighting suit. "Here is your helmet," said Lance. He handed it to her. "We must go!"

Kasey glanced at Wyatt. His gloomy expression broke her heart. "What are you going to do?" he asked. "I want to go with you, but I can't," he said. "You have to choose."

Kasey took her helmet from Lance. She put it on and turned to face Wyatt. "I'm sorry," she said. "I have to go. This is what I do. This is what you should do." Wyatt faded from sight. Kasey followed Lance and Chief Carpenter out of the ball room.

The dream ended as Kasey rubbed her tired eyes. She pulled her blanket up to her chin and forced herself to sit up. Tiger, her striped cat, hopped onto the bed and rubbed itself against her. The purring rang in the air.

"Good morning, Tiger," said Kasey. She rubbed the top of the cat's head. The animal flopped onto the blanket. "I envy you pal," said Kasey. "You are blissfully unaware of anything happening outside this apartment. No wars, no famine, no economic strife." She gently touched one of its legs. "No love life."

Kasey sighed. "Do you want to hear about my problems?" she asked. The cat waved its tail in the air. "I really like Lance. He's smart, sweet, and lots of fun. But I also like Wyatt. I don't really know him, but he is dark and brooding, and you know how hot that is."

Kasey got out of bed and Tiger followed her to the bathroom. "And the worst part? They are both firefighters. Well, one is, and one was. It's complicated." She washed her face and continued her conversation. "I know. I don't date firefighters." She looked down at the cat. "So, what am I supposed to do?"

The cat mellowed and circled around Kasey. "You want breakfast, don't you?" Kasey left the bathroom and walked to the tiny kitchen in her apartment. She filled Tiger's food bowl and poured water into another bowl. Tiger chomped on the food.

"You're a big help, fella," said Kasey.

****

The firetruck screeched to a halt in front of the warehouse building. Flames ate away at the three-story structure. Police officers held back the curious crowd. Kasey and Lance hopped off the truck and connected fire hoses to nearby fire hydrants.

Kasey saw her father emerge from the captain's vehicle. A police officer approached the captain and led him to a man in a business suit. Kasey rushed over to find out what was going on. She stopped behind her father and listened to the man in the suit.

"No one should be in there at this hour," said the man. He pointed to an older man dressed in a blue shirt and matching pants. "Our security guard got out. He's fine. He told me that he didn't see anyone. He has no idea how this started."

The captain turned and saw Kasey. "You and Lance do one sweep and get out. Hopefully no one is hiding in there." Kasey nodded. "And be careful," said the captain. "If this was set on purpose, the purp could still be nearby."

Kasey ran back toward Lance and relayed the captain's message. They checked their equipment before rushing inside the inferno.

The thick smoke cut down on visibility. Kasey made a point of staying close to Lance. They checked several offices, calling out to anyone who might be there. The duo worked quickly. Kasey got a call on her radio. "Carpenter, have you found anyone?" asked the fire chief.

Kasey responded. "No sir. No one yet. We are finishing the first floor. Should we proceed to the second floor?" she asked.

"Negative," replied the captain. "Get out as soon as you finish floor one."

Lance turned toward Kasey and pointed in the direction they arrived. Kasey knew that meant that Lance heard the captain's message too. Kasey led the pullout with Lance on her heels. The firefighters pushed past fallen debris and quickly made their way outside again.

Kasey and Lance helped their crewmates hose down the warehouse. After the flames died out, Kasey strode over to her father. The captain stood with Deputy Colin James and Sheriff Blake Hughes. The men looked worried.

Kasey shook Colin's hand. "Deputy James," she said. "Nice to see you."

Colin nodded and let go of her hand. "I wish it was under better circumstances."

Kasey frowned. "We got the fire out and no one was hurt," she said. "I'd say those are pretty good circumstances." She looked at her father, and then at the sheriff. Both men had their arms crossed over their chests. "Am I missing something?" asked Kasey.

Chief Carpenter leaned toward his daughter. "Several empty kerosene containers were found behind the warehouse," he said. "Just like the church fire."

Sheriff Hughes summed up what they were all thinking. "It looks like Penn Hills has a serial arsonist in its midst." He glanced at Colin. "So far, no one has been hurt." He looked over at Chief Carpenter. "We haven't had a case like this in decades. We are going to need all the help we can get."

"You have the full cooperation of the fire department," said Carpenter. "Anything you need, you just ask for," he said. He shook the sheriff's hand. The lawmen turned and walked toward the rear of the building. Carpenter faced his daughter. “This could get ugly very quickly,” he said. “We need to find this person before the town falls prey to a witch hunt.”

****

Kasey pushed the wobbly shopping cart down the supermarket aisle and scanned the shelves for cat food. She knew that Tiger was picky and would only eat one brand of food. The store aisles had been renovated and Kasey had trouble finding that brand. She nearly gave up when she finally saw what she needed at far end of the aisle. Kasey picked up two 10-pound bags and put them in her cart.

She turned toward the bread section when she saw Wyatt James standing next to a small cart. Kasey smiled and nervously pushed her cart toward him. She saw him pick up a loaf of pumpernickel bread. He studied it for a moment. “That’s a bold choice,” she said. He looked up at her and smiled. “Most people get white or wheat, or maybe rye. But few people are brave enough to eat pumpernickel bread,” she said.

Wyatt shook his head, clearly confused. “It’s just bread,” he said. “And it’s twice as much as the other stuff.” He lifted the package closer to his face. “Are there little prizes in there or something?” he asked.

“None that I know of,” said Kasey. She took the loaf from him and examined it before she handed it back to him. “Sorry, no prizes.” She leaned on her cart handle and smiled. “It’s nice to see a masculine guy like you food shopping.”

“He else would I eat?” asked Wyatt. He peeked into her cart. “You have a cat,” he said. Kasey nodded. “Any roommates or boyfriends?” he asked.

Kasey tilted her head. "Why, that's mighty presumptuous of you to ask, since you are obviously involved with someone." Kasey smiled. "How would Susan react?" she asked.

"I'm not sure," said Wyatt. He folded his arms across his chest. "Especially since we agreed to keep things casual." His smile faded. "I read about the warehouse fire," he said. "It doesn't appear to be an accident, does it?" he asked.

Kasey moved closer to him and lowered her voice. "No. We found empty kerosene containers behind the warehouse. Just like at the church." She looked around before continuing. "My dad and the sheriff think we have a serial arsonist in town."

The wind came out of Wyatt's sails. "Oh no," he said. "Not again."

"Not again?" asked Kasey.

Wyatt swallowed hard. "Two years ago in Ohio, the small county I lived in was terrorized by a serial arsonist. The perp had the entire community on edge for four mounts until he surrendered to police. One of the perp's family members turned him in. When the cops asked him why he did it, he said that he likes to see things burn."

Wyatt shook his head. "How are we supposed to fight against that?" he asked.

"By not giving up," said Kasey. "By investigating all the leads until something breaks the case. Firebugs are like most criminals. They have a reason for doing it, and they usually make mistakes. That's how we catch them."

Wyatt rubbed his red eyes. "I wish I had your confidence," he said. "Not that it matters," he added. "My firefighting days might be over."

"Why is that?" asked Kasey.

"I'd rather not talk about it," said Wyatt. He pushed his cart a few feet down the aisle. He picked up a package and turned toward Kasey. "What do you know about bagels?" he asked.

Kasey laughed and took the package of bagels from him. "They are really bad for you, but they taste amazing," she said. "Especially with cream cheese." She put the bagels in his cart. "C'mon," she said. "The Dairy section is this way," she said.

Kasey guided Wyatt through the store and provided commentary on most of his purchases. They paid for their food and headed for the exit. "Do you mind walking me to my car?" she asked. She leaned into him. "It's nice to have a big, strong man around to protect me," she said. Kasey held a straight face for a few seconds before she burst into laughter.

They walked to Kasey's car, where Wyatt loaded her bags into the rear of the vehicle. "My hero," she teased, after he finished. They smiled at each other as they awkwardly stood behind her car. "You know, nothing in my car will melt in this nice weather," she said. "Would you like to join me for a cup of coffee?" she asked.

"I would," said Wyatt. He pointed to his own cart of food. "Stay here a moment and I'll come back after I load up my car," he suggested. Kasey agreed and she watched Wyatt push his cart toward his car. She couldn't keep her eyes off his tight behind as he moved away from her.

Wyatt followed Kasey's car until she pulled into the parking lot of a local coffee house. He parked next to her vehicle and walked inside with her. They found an empty table and sat down across from each other. "I didn't know this place was still here," said Wyatt. "I thought it would have been converted to a Starbucks years ago."

"Shhh," said Kasey, with a raised finger to her lips. "We don't say the S-word here," she joked. She picked up a menu from the table and looked it over. Wyatt did the same.

Wyatt shook his head. “Would it be wrong to order a regular coffee with two sugars?” he asked. “I don’t want to look out of place.” He put his menu down and smiled at Kasey.

“Order whatever you want,” said Kasey. “My treat.” She looked at the menu again. After a moment, she put the menu down. “A regular coffee sounds good.”

A waitress came over and took their orders. The young girl rolled her eyes at their choices and dashed back to the deliver the news to the baristas.

“She did not look impressed,” said Wyatt. “Was it something I said?”

Kasey shook her head. “No, she’s just too young to understand the value of a great cup of regular coffee.” She folded her hands and rested them on the table. “It’s a nice break from the swill we have at the fire station. With so many drinkers to serve, we can’t afford the good stuff on our budget.”

“Is that supposed to be a selling point?” asked Wyatt.

“Of course,” replied Kasey. “Free, lousy coffee is a perk of the job.”

Wyatt sat back in his seat as his expression darkened. “Is that why we’re here?” he asked. “So you could try and recruit me again?” he asked. He took a deep breath and glared at her.

“No, not at all,” said Kasey. She reached out and touched his right hand. “I invited you here because I wanted to spend time with you. That’s all.” She paused and added a little more truth. “I kinda had a thing for you in high school.” She looked down at the table. “I never had the guts to tell you then.” She raised her eyes to him. “I didn’t want to let another chance get away.”

Wyatt smiled. “I didn’t know that then,” he said. “I wish I had.”

Kasey held her breath. She stared at Wyatt and wondered what his next move would be. He appeared to be mulling it over. Kasey slowly let her breath out. She clenched her hands and hid them under the table. She felt like a schoolgirl, and she had the sweaty palms to prove it.

"Hey Kasey," said someone behind her. She dejectedly turned to see who it was. Her eyes widened when she saw Lance holding a Styrofoam cup in his left hand. "I thought it was you." He smiled at her before turning to face Wyatt. "You must be Wyatt James," said Lance. He offered a hand. "I've heard a lot about you." The men shook hands. "I'm Lance Davis. I work with Kasey at the firehouse."

"It's nice to meet you," said Wyatt. He let go of Lance's hand. "Would you like to join us?" asked Wyatt. He looked over his shoulder. "We can grab another chair."

"No, that won't be necessary," said Lance. "I got my coffee to go." He addressed Kasey. "I gotta run. I'll see you later at the station." He pivoted and walked toward the exit.

"Don't worry," said Wyatt. "That wasn't awkward at all."

The waitress came over with their coffees. She placed them in front of Kasey and Wyatt before she took off.

Wyatt picked up his cup and sipped the coffee. "Very good," he said. "Better than the swill we had in Ohio."

Kasey picked up her cup and drank. She nodded. "Definitely better than our cheap stuff at the station." She drank more. "You are still invited to visit sometime, if you like."

Wyatt shrugged. "Maybe," he replied. He rubbed his eyes. "How did you get into the firefighting business?" he asked. He drank more coffee.

Kasey smiled. “It’s not a very original story,” she said. “My father was a firefighter, and he told me lots of stories growing up about what he did for a living.” She lifted her eyebrows. “It sounded exciting, so I took junior classes until I was old enough to join our department.”

“And now your dad is the fire chief,” said Wyatt. He lifted his cup toward his face so he could smell the coffee. The scent made him smile. “That must cause some friction at home.”

Kasey shook her head. “No, we actually get along well.” She shuffled in her seat until she found a comfortable spot. “I think we really bonded after my mother left us. It brought us closer together.” She drank more coffee. “Sometimes we get on each other’s nerves, but that happens with anyone that you live with.”

“You are lucky,” said Wyatt. “My father and I argue all the time. Thank God Colin is there, or one of us would be jail,” said Wyatt. He finished his drink. “I wish my dad and I got along better, but nothing I do seems good enough for him. It never did.”

Kasey gently placed a hand on his. “I’m sorry to hear that,” she said. She gave his hand a quick squeeze. “Sometimes it helps to talk about it.” She shrugged. “If you want to, I’ll listen.”

Wyatt shook his head. “Not right now,” he said. “Not on a date.”

Kasey perked up. “Is that what this is?” she asked. “A date?”

“I’d like to think so,” said Wyatt. He pushed his cup aside and looked into her eyes.

Kasey leaned toward him a bit more aggressively. Nothing was going to stop her from kissing him this time. Their lips were nearly touching when Kasey’s phone rang. It was her father’s ringtone. She sat back again and let out a small moan. “I’m sorry, it’s my dad,” she said. “It’s probably important.” Wyatt nodded and sat back.

"Hey Dad," said Kasey into her phone. "What? When did that happen? Really? Okay, I'll be right there," she said. She closed her phone and sighed. "The police have a suspect in custody for the arson fires," she said. "My dad wants me to meet him at the police station."

Kasey grabbed her purse and took out a few dollars out of her wallet. Wyatt put his right hand up in protest. "Don't worry about that," he said. "I'll get the bill." Kasey stuffed the money back into her wallet. "Would you like me to go with you?" he asked.

"No, that's alright," said Kasey. She laughed. "I've never had a date end in jail. Best not to push my luck." She leaned forward and quickly kissed Wyatt's right cheek. "I will call you later," she said. Kasey paused and looked at Wyatt one more time before she dashed to the door.

****

Kasey nervously rubbed her hands together as a police officer led her to the rear of the station. The officer opened a door and stepped aside. Kasey entered the room and saw her father and the sheriff peering through a one-way pane of glass.

"What is she doing here, Sam?" asked the sheriff.

"She is my guest, Blake," said Fire Chief Carpenter. Kasey's dad waved her over to the glass. "This guy is really nervous," he said. "He is definitely guilty of something. Look at the way he rocks back and forth in his chair. He knows we have him."

"We don't have anything yet, Sam," said the sheriff.

Colin entered the room with a file in his hand, and he nodded at the sheriff. "I think he's sweat for long enough," he said. "It's time to grill him." Colin paused to collect himself. "Any suggestions, Sheriff?"

The senior lawman patted Colin on the shoulder. “Establish your dominance right off the bat,” he said. “And no matter what he says or does, act like you were anticipating it. Don’t look surprised or confused. Don’t give him any power.”

Kasey watched Colin exit their room and reappear in the next room. Colin casually sat down across the suspect. Kasey whispered to her dad. “Who is this guy?” she asked. “What do we have on him.?”

The fire chief responded without taking his eyes off the suspect. “His name is Joey Long. He grew up in Philly before moving here two years ago. He’s got a long rap sheet, including busts for setting small fires on private property.” The chief glanced at his daughter. “Guess what he used to start those fires.”

Kasey nodded. “Kerosene,” she said. She watched Colin as he sat quietly staring at Joey Long. The sheriff turned a knob up so they all could clearly hear the conversation.

Colin opened the file and placed photos in front of Joey. “These are pictures we took of the church and the warehouse that you tried to burn down.” Joey averted his eyes. Colin slammed the table with his fist and pointed to the photos. “Look at them, Joey,” he said. “Look at your handiwork.”

Joey pushed the pictures toward Colin. “No, man, you got it all wrong,” said Joey. “I didn’t do this. Why would I burn these two places down?” he asked. “I’m not even sure where they are.”

Colin leaned toward Joey. “You know where they are. They’re five blocks from your home, Joey,” said Colin. “You probably pass them every day.” He paused and scratched his neck. “Someone offer you money to do this?” he asked.

"No," said Joey. "Like I told you, I don't need money. My folks have plenty." Joey looked over Colin's shoulder. "Is that two-way glass?" he asked. Colin didn't respond. "Whose watching us?" asked Joey.

"Are you a religious man, Joey?" asked Colin. He pushed the photos back toward the suspect. "Do you go to church every Sunday?" Joey shook his head. "Well maybe you should find religion because God is watching you. He knows every move you make." Colin leaned toward Joey. "You don't want to piss off God, do you?"

"You're full of it," replied Joey. He leaned back in his seat. "God doesn't have time to worry about a punk like me," he said.

"That's the first smart thing you've said," asserted Colin. "You are right. God wouldn't waste his time on a loser like you." He picked up a picture of the burnt church. "Was this your way of getting God's attention?" he asked.

Joey said nothing.

Colin put the photograph down and he picked up one of the warehouse pictures. "Whose attention were you trying to get here?" he asked. "Could it be the manager who fired you recently? You used to work at this place until they let you go."

Joe's face whitened.

Colin put that picture down. "That's right Joey" he said. "We know all about your work history. You don't last too long on jobs. You were only at the warehouse for 3 weeks." Colin stood and walked around the table. He stopped behind the suspect. "You like fires, don't you? You like to see things go up in flames. That gets you going somehow. You are one sick bastard."

"I didn't do this," said Joey. He crossed his arms over his chest. "I'm done talking. I want to see my lawyer."

Colin collected the pictures and put them back in the file. He stood and left Joey Long in the interrogation room. He entered the second room and handed the file to the sheriff. "He went to the lawyer too quickly," he said. "This guy is dirty."

Sheriff Hughes put the file in his briefcase. "He probably is, but we don't have much to hold him on right now." He locked the briefcase. "Colin, I thought you said you could crack this guy," said Hughes. "What happened?"

Colin shrugged. "He asked for a lawyer. I have to stop at that point."

The sheriff shook his head. "You brought him in too early, Colin. You should have waited until we had a stronger case." He stood face to face with his deputy. "Now he has time to dump any evidence we might have found. Damn sloppy police work, Deputy James," he said.

"We can hold him for 72 hours," said Colin. "That should be enough time to strengthen our case," he said.

"And if it is not?" asked the sheriff. "Then what?"

Colin took a deep breath and let it out slowly. "He is our guy. He had motive and opportunity. After his lawyer gets here, I'll go at him again." He turned and stormed out of the room.

Kasey watched Sheriff Hughes turn to face the fire chief. "I like Colin," said Hughes. "He has a bright future here but has a lot to learn." He shook Chief Carpenter's hand before he looked at Kasey. “I would appreciate it if you could talk some sense into him. Maybe he will listen to you.”

Chapter Five

Wyatt downshifted and applied the clutch and brake as the old Ford pickup truck slowed to a stop. Wyatt looked both ways at the intersection before easing the truck forward. It was still dark and there were few vehicles on the roads. He glanced over at his father, whose grumpy disposition had not changed.

"You missed the turn," said David James. He shook his head. "You never were good at directions." He glared at Wyatt. "How did you ever find your way to the fires?" He pointed to the road they had just crossed. "That was Crockett Drive," he said. "You were supposed to turn right onto Crockett."

Wyatt slowed his breathing and tried not to let his father upset him. "Dad, that was Milner Ave, not Crockett," he said. "Crockett is still three miles away. Where the Sunoco gas station used to be."

"Don't sass me, boy!" shouted David. "I've been going to this fishing hole long before you were born," he said. He turned his head toward the rear of the truck. "I'm telling you that was our turn. Now we're going to be late getting there and all the good fishing spots will be taken." He faced his son again. "Are you going to turn around and go back, or are we just going to drive around aimlessly all day?"

"I'm not turning around because we haven't missed our turn," snapped Wyatt.

"You really are a moron," said David. He elbowed the passenger side door. "Why did I agree to this trip anyway? You don't know the first thing about fishing. I'll spend the whole day teaching you what a normal eight-year-old boy already knows."

Wyatt focused on the road and tried to drown out his father's voice. He thought about turning on the radio, but that would give David something else to complain about. Wyatt had suggested this trip the day before and he should have known it was a bad idea when it took Colin to get their father to agree to it. Wyatt asked Colin to join them, but he was busy working on a major police case.

They finally came upon Crockett Drive, and Wyatt slowly turned onto the road and pointed at the street sign. "See Dad," he said. "This is where we turn." Wyatt straightened the wheel as the Ford chugged along the road. David mumbled something as he looked out the passenger-side window.

Daylight finally broke as Wyatt pulled into a parking spot. He quietly got out of the truck and moved toward the vehicle's rear. He pulled down the tailgate and grabbed some of their equipment. He saw his father coming toward him. David picked up his weather-beaten red tackle box and his aging fishing rod. "Follow me," he ordered.

Wyatt carried the gear as he followed his father to their favorite spot along the river. He set the gear on a dry rockface. Wyatt checked his pants and boots. They were tight enough to keep out most of the chilly water.

David opened his tackle box and threaded bait onto his fishing line. He stepped into the murky water and cast his line. The lessons he was to teach Wyatt were forgotten about. The old man stood still with his fishing rod in his hands.

Wyatt wanted to thank his father for coming on the trip, but he knew that total silence was expected now. He quietly removed some bait from David's tackle box and put it on his fishing line. Wyatt entered the water but kept six feet between himself and his father as he cast his line. It landed with a thump that echoed around them. Wyatt cringed and waited for a reprimand from his father, but fortunately none came forth.

An hour passed before either of them had so much as a nibble. Wyatt's legs began to tire, but he remained standing in his spot. He knew that if he tried to sit down, his father would berate him, so he sucked in a deep breath and tried to ignore the pain. Wyatt slowly shifted his weight from foot to foot to relieve some of the discomfort.

Other fishermen arrived and departed as the hours dragged on. Wyatt politely nodded at them but was careful not to speak. He watched his father ignore the others, unless one of them came too close to his fishing area. Those few unfortunate souls got an earful of obscenities until they cleared out. Wyatt cringed each time his father fired a salvo of nasty words at the strangers.

The mid-day sun did little to change their luck, or David's bad mood. Wyatt stretched his arms toward the sky and yawned. He sloshed his way to the bank of the river and sat down on the dry land. Wyatt opened the basket of food he had prepared the night before. He unwrapped a ham sandwich and quietly ate his lunch.

Wyatt picked up another sandwich and he waved his right hand at his father. David looked over at his son and he finally gave in to his hunger and fatigue. David stomped his feet as he exited the lake and sat down near his son. Wyatt handed David the sandwich and remained quiet. He didn't want his father interrupting the beautiful silence of Nature.

"No damn luck today," said David. He chewed his food and wiped his mouth with the back of his hand. "The water must be too cold. That's why we're not catching anything." He took another bite of his sandwich.

Wyatt wanted to point to the other fishermen who had caught a good number of fish, but he didn't want to upset his father. He finished his light lunch and put the trash inside the basket. Wyatt leaned against a tree and watched two squirrels dart across the high branches. He smiled and wished that he were having that much fun.

"Here, take this," said David, as he handed his trash to Wyatt. "We don't want to litter." David found his own tree to lean against. "It is so beautiful here," he said. "So peaceful and calm. You won't find a place like this anywhere else in the world." He shuffled to get more comfortable. "I'll never leave this area. And if you were smart, Wyatt, you'd stay her too. Penn Hills is a nice place to raise a family."

Wyatt chuckled. "You sound like a tourist commercial," he said. David didn't laugh. "It's okay to smile, Dad," said Wyatt. "It won't scare away the fish."

"I'll smile when I want to," said David. "And what of it? What do I have to smile about at this point in my life?" He looked over at the water. "I'm old, my wife is gone, and I'm stuck talking to people I don't like. What the Hell kind of life is that?" he asked.

"Dad, c'mon," said Wyatt. "It's not that bad. You've got friends who care about you. And you have two sons who love you," said Wyatt. "That sounds alright to me."

David shook his head. "I miss my wife," he said. "She was my whole world. When she died, most of me died too." He wiped his eyes with his right hand. "You wouldn't understand that. You're young, and you haven't loved a woman the way I loved her."

Wyatt waited a moment before responding. "I miss her too, Dad," he said. "We all do." He sat up and rested his hands on his knees. "I know how important she was to you, and I'm sorry that she won't be here anymore."

"You're sorry?" asked David. "You miss her?" He removed his fishing cap and wiped sweat from his face and head before putting the hat back on. "But you didn't miss her enough when she was alive to come and visit her. You didn't see the heartbreak on her face when she realized that you weren't here." He picked up a stone and tossed it into the water. "No, you were too busy, even when you knew she was sick. And I was left to pick up the pieces."

"Enough!" shouted Wyatt. He shot to his feet and glared at his father. "I know I was wrong not to visit her. You don't need to keep throwing that in my face." Wyatt saw other fishermen look over at him. He lowered his voice. "I'm sorry for the trouble my absence caused. But badgering me about it won't change anything, so knock it off."

David rose and stepped toward Wyatt. They stood inches apart. "How dare you tell me what to do," said David. "I was with her every day. I watched her deteriorate right before my eyes. She was the love of my life and there was nothing I could do to help her. But I was there."

David turned and marched away from his son. Wyatt raised his hands in frustration. "Where are you going?" he asked. David continued without looking back. "Fine. I'll get all our stuff together," said Wyatt. He packed up their gear and carried it toward the truck.

Wyatt loaded the gear in the back of the Ford as David sat in the passenger seat. Wyatt hopped into the driver's seat and closed the door. He sat still for a moment to give his father a chance to say something. David remained quiet. Wyatt turned the ignition key and backed the truck out of the parking spot.

Neither spoke as the truck rambled over the road. They were a few miles from home when Wyatt saw a car pulled over on the side of the road. The vehicle's hazard lights flashed. Wyatt pulled the truck over and stopped behind the vehicle. He got out and saw someone trying to change a flat tire. The person struggled with removing the lug nuts. "Hello," said Wyatt, as he slowly approached the person. "Can I give you a hand?" he asked.

"I hope so," said the person. She turned around and Wyatt recognized Kasey Carpenter's face. Her cheeks were red from exertion, and she had grease on her hands. She smiled as he got closer. She handed him the lug wrench. "Normally I can do this myself," said Kasey. "But they are really on."

Wyatt saw his father get out of the truck. David stood beside Kasey, as Wyatt leaned down and examined the problem. He put the wrench on one lug to get a feel for it. "You're going to need to stand on the wrench to get it going," said David.

"Thanks Dad," said Wyatt. He positioned himself beside the vehicle and pushed on the wrench with his right foot. The nut didn't move. He pumped his foot until he loosened the nut. Wyatt unscrewed the nut and put it into his pocket.

"Be careful not to lose that thing," said David. Wyatt glared at his father. David turned to face Kasey. "That boy is always losing stuff," he said. "I remember when he was 11 . . ."

"I think he is doing fine," said Kasey, as she cut David off. She gently put a hand on David's right shoulder. "It's cold out here, Mr. James. Maybe you would be more comfortable waiting in your truck," she said.

David took the hint and walked back to his own vehicle.

"Thank you for that," said Wyatt. He loosened the other lug nuts and Kasey helped him remove the flat tire. Wyatt replaced it with the spare and tightened that wheel on. Wyatt put the damaged tire in the trunk. "You are all set," he said.

Kasey leaned forward and hugged Wyatt. "You are my hero," said Kasey. She quickly kissed his left cheek. "How can I make it up to you?" she asked.

Wyatt waved his right hand. "No need to," he said. "I'm glad to help."

"I insist," said Kasey. "Come to the fire house tonight," she said. "It's my turn to make dinner, and I'm making chicken cordon bleu." Wyatt shrugged. "C'mon, you'll love it. And you can meet the guys," she said.

"Still trying to recruit me?" asked Wyatt. He put his hands on his hips.

Kasey snuggled in toward him. "No," she said. "I'm trying to get another date with you." Kasey laughed. "Boy, you are really not good at flirting, are you?" She kissed his cheek again. "We eat at 7, so come by before then."

Wyatt gently touched her chin. "I'd love to, but Colin and I are taking my dad out to dinner tonight," he said. Kasey frowned. "Don't sulk. We can do it another night," he said.

Kasey playfully pushed him away. "Okay. Another night. But make it soon."

David honked the truck's horn. Wyatt looked over at him. "Let's go!" yelled David. "I want to get home and get changed."

Wyatt turned back to Kasey. "I have to go," he said.

Kasey nodded. "I see that," she said. "Go take care of your dad. I'll see you soon."

Wyatt climbed back into the Ford and watched Kasey safely pull her car onto the road. He eased the truck forward and continued toward his childhood home. David turned on the radio and moved the dial to a jazz station. Wyatt tapped his fingers on the steering wheel as he thought about his emerging relationship with Kasey.

****

The James brothers stood outside the restaurant and waited for the father to join them. Wyatt looked at Colin and shook his head. "Well, that was a disaster," said Wyatt. He bit down on a toothpick that he got from the eatery. "I don't know why I even try with him," said Wyatt. "Nothing is ever good enough. Nothing ever will be."

Colin put his right hand on Wyatt's shoulder. "Cut him some slack, Wyatt," said Colin. He pulled his hand back and slid it into his coat pocket. "He just lost his wife, the only woman he has ever loved. He is devastated."

"I know that," replied Wyatt. "He won't let me forget that, or the fact that I wasn't here for her." He quickly rubbed his temples. "I've apologized to him till I'm blue in the face. It doesn't matter. Dad obviously doesn't want me here. I should just go back to Ohio."

"And do what?" asked Colin, "You've made it clear that you don't want to be a firefighter anymore." Wyatt started to respond, but Colin cut him off. "I know you are having doubts about yourself, but don't think for a minute that Dad doesn't love you. He's hurting and he needs both of his sons right now."

Wyatt sighed and nodded. "He just makes it so difficult to be around him."

"Maybe you just need a break," said Colin. "Why don't you take that bike of yours out for a spin?" he asked. "It's been cluttering up our garage for years. Change the oil, put some new gas in it, and take it for a ride. It will help you clear your head."

Wyatt smiled. "That's a great idea, Colin," he said. He lightly punched his brother's right shoulder. "Sometimes you are not so dumb," he added. They both laughed.

Colin drove the truck home from the restaurant, which gave Wyatt a chance to sit in the back by himself. David and Colin chatted about dinner while Wyatt closed his eyes and thought about his love life. Susan had called him a few times, but he kept the conversations short and avoided making plans with her. He really wanted to be with Kasey, but he couldn't tell if she were interested in him as a boyfriend or just another firefighter for her squad.

Wyatt opened the garage door as Colin escorted their father inside their home. Wyatt smiled as he pulled the cover off his Honda motorcycle. The 250cc machine was a street-legal dirt bike with thick tires and a comfortable seat. Wyatt folded the cover and put in on a nearby shelf.

Wyatt drained the old oil into a pan before storing the brown liquid in a container. He made a mental note to bring the used oil to a shop for proper disposal. He repeated the process by emptying out the gas tank. Wyatt found unopened cans of oil on shelf near the back of the garage, and he put the right amount into the bike. Finally, he refilled the gas tank with fuel from another steel container.

The rider checked the spark plugs before he rolled the machine out onto the driveway. He pressed the electric start, and, after a few tries, his motorcycle roared to life. Wyatt put on his helmet and sat down on the bike. He gripped the handlebar and slightly turned the throttle. The motorcycle roared again, as if beckoning him to ride it.

Wyatt turned on the vehicle's lights before he shifted into first gear and eased out the clutch. The motorcycle moved forward, and it took the rider a moment to get his balance back. Once on the street, it all came back to Wyatt. His instincts kicked in and he rode the machine faster and faster along his neighborhood streets.

The tour allowed Wyatt to see more of his beloved hometown. He sped past the shopping center packed with pedestrians that shuffled from store to store. He crossed over Main Street and rode along Hamilton Drive toward his old high school. Wyatt glided into the parking lot before he turned around and headed further South along Adams Avenue.

Wyatt stopped at Washington Park and pulled into a parking spot. He turned off his machine and walked in the near-darkness toward the playground area. He smiled at the swing sets and the jungle gyms that he and Colin played on when they were kids. The light poles shinned down on the popular carousel that sat in the middle of the park.

Feeling nostalgic, Wyatt climbed up on the carousel and sat on a silver horse. He placed his hands on the grips and pretended that the steed was galloping across an open field. He could hear the horseshoes clopping along the ground as the wind whipped across his face. The laughter of children filled his ears. Wyatt closed his eyes and imagined that he was eight-years-old again, and that park was filled with happy patrons.

Wyatt's eyes grew heavily. He rested his head on his hands and he promptly fell asleep.

Wyatt was back in Ohio. He and his fire-fighting crew pushed their way through a burning house, looking for anyone that hadn't made it out yet. They had cleared all but one room in the house, and Wyatt led the way into the last bedroom. He carefully opened the door and flashed his light around the room. Wyatt saw something move in the far corner. He rushed over and found a man lying face-down on the floor. He gently rolled the man onto his back.

The firefighter snapped back when he saw the charred face of his brother, Colin James. The victim spoke softly, and it was difficult to hear him over the flames. Colin repeated his words as loudly as he could. "Why did you leave me here?" he asked.

Chapter Six

Wyatt shouted as he violently awoke from his nightmare. He looked around, confused, having no idea where he was or how he got there. He tried to control his breathing. In and out, slowly. He rubbed his eyes and looked around. The silver horse was still underneath him, and similar figures surrounded him.

Wyatt nodded as the pieces began to fit together. He dismounted the horse and gingerly lowered himself off the carousel. Darkness swallowed the town and the only light he could see was manmade. He stumbled across the wet grass until he found his motorcycle. Wyatt slowly put on his helmet and fired up his ride.

His senses finally returned to normal, so he carefully released the clutch and turned the throttle toward himself. The bike lunged forward and wobbled until Wyatt gained full control of it. He passed lit houses and familiar landmarks as he sped home on the lonely streets.

The rider turned onto his street and stopped when he saw four police cars parked outside his home with their lights flashing. He revved his engine and took off toward the congregation of government vehicles.

Wyatt glided onto the driveway and turned off the engine. Two police officers moved toward him. "What's going on here?" asked Wyatt. He stopped his bike and rested it on the kickstand. "Is anyone hurt?" He tried to move passed the men, but they cut him off.

"Slow down, Wyatt," said the taller officer. He put his hands up and grabbed Wyatt's jacket. "We just want to talk to you." The lawman roughly pushed Wyatt to slow his momentum. "There's nothing to worry about."

Wyatt tried to wiggle free. The shorter cop grabbed his arms from behind. "Take it easy, Wyatt," he said. "We don't want to hurt you. We are only here to talk." The lawman tightened his grip as Wyatt refused to settle down.

The taller officer pushed his face a few inches from Wyatt's. "Mr. James," he said, over pronouncing the name. "This will not help you. You need to stop this." Both officers led him to the front porch, where they sat him on a bench. The taller officer stayed with him, while his partner went inside.

Sweat rolled down Wyatt's face that he could only blink away. The other officer returned with Colin and Sheriff Hughes on his heels. "Let go of him!" shouted Colin. He raced over to Wyatt to check on him. "Are you alright?" he asked.

Wyatt nodded. "Yeah, I'm fine." His face whitened. "Is it Dad?" he asked. "Did something happen to him?" He felt his eyes well up. "Where is he?" he asked.

Colin gently put both of his hands on his brother's shoulders. "Listen to me," said the lawman. "Dad is fine. I'm fine. That's not why the police are here." He paused, as if searching for the right words. "We are all here for you," he said.

Wyatt shook his head. "I don't understand," he replied. "For me?"

Sheriff Hughes stood before Wyatt. "We want to ask you some questions," he said.

Wyatt shrugged. "Okay. Ask me." He glanced at Colin, but the deputy's stony expression gave nothing away. Wyatt looked back at Hughes.

"Where were you tonight?" asked Hughes. He glared at Wyatt as if he were talking to a convicted killer. "Over the last two hours." He leaned toward Wyatt. The sheriff was two inches taller and forty pounds heavier than Wyatt, and his attempt at intimidation was succeeding.

Wyatt shrugged. "I was riding around on my motorcycle," he said. He looked around at the uniformed bystanders as panic began to set in. "Am I in trouble here?" he asked.

"Why would you ask that, Wyatt?" asked Hughes. His eyes darted from Colin to Wyatt. "Do you have something you want to tell us?" He removed a small notebook from his coat pocket. A pencil soon followed in his left hand.

"No," replied Wyatt. "I just want to know what is happening here?"

Colin stepped toward his brother. "There was another fire tonight, Wyatt," he said softly. "At Zorbis Bar. While Joey Long was in custody." The deputy sighed. "We didn't have much on him to begin with. We had to release him." He patted Wyatt's right shoulder.

"So, now you're looking at me for this?" asked Wyatt. He took a step toward the sheriff, forcing the officers to intervene. The tall cop put both of his hands on Wyatt's upper body. "That's crap and you know it!" yelled Wyatt. "I'm a firefighter! I've risked my life countless times putting out fires."

Hughes nodded and tapped the pencil against the notebook. "And maybe you helped some of those fires get started," he said. He puffed his chest out. "Give you the chance to be the big hero." He paused and glared at Wyatt. "It has occurred to us that these fires all happened after you came back to town."

"That's pretty flimsy, sheriff," replied Wyatt.

Hughes pointed to the garage. "We searched your house, with your father's permission, and we found containers filled with kerosene in the garage," he said. "Funny though, you don't own any kerosene heaters. That's what your father told us."

"In a town like this, anyone could have planted them there," said Wyatt. He rubbed his cold hands together. "Most folks around here don't even lock their doors at night. It would be easy to slip into a garage and leave anything behind."

Hughes shook his head. "Now that's pretty flimsy," he replied. He jotted down some notes before putting the notebook back in his coat pocket. "Mr. James, we'd like you to come down to the station with us to continue this conversation."

"Do I have a choice?" asked Wyatt.

"Yes, you can come nicely, or in handcuffs," said Hughes. He took a pair off the beltloop of his pants. He clanged the metal circles together. "What will it be?" he asked.

Wyatt turned toward his brother. "Colin, you guys can't be serious," he pleaded.

Colin took a step away from Wyatt. "It doesn't look good," he said. He tilted his head. "Maybe you did this, maybe you didn't. We don't know for sure, but we can't take any chances. We have to protect the people in this town." He swallowed hard. "I'm sorry."

Sheriff Hughes nodded toward the tall officer, who forcefully turned Wyatt around. Hughes placed the handcuffs on Wyatt's wrists. "I'm sorry, too, Wyatt," he said. "But I have to be sure that you won't try anything on the way to the station." He pushed Wyatt past the others and marched him toward his police cruiser.

The interrogation room smelled like coffee and urine. Florescent light poured down from the ceiling. Wyatt sat with his hands cuffed to a ring at the edge of a table. His tired eyes ached, and he struggled to keep them open. The police officers left him alone in this room for more than an hour. Wyatt knew they were trying to break his spirit.

Sheriff Hughes finally entered the room with a folder in his hands. He sat down across from Wyatt. Hughes dropped the folder in front of Wyatt, and it slammed against the tabletop. "You look awful, Wyatt," said Hughes. "You need to get some sleep."

"Let me out of here and I'll do just that," said Wyatt. He blinked and looked behind Hughes. "Where is Colin?" he asked. "He should be in here. He knows I would never do anything like this."

"Your brother is temporarily off the case," said Hughes. He opened the file and pulled pictures out. "Conflict of interest," said Hughes. "I'm sure you can see why." He placed photographs on the table in front of Wyatt. "Look at all this destruction. All this senseless property loss." He shook his head. "So far, you've been lucky. No one has been hurt. But how long can your luck hold out?" he asked.

Wyatt leaned back in his chair. "I didn't do any of this, and you know it," he said. "I know what you are doing."

Hughes lowered his eyebrows. "What is it that you think I'm doing?" he asked.

"You're looking for a quick way to close this case," said Wyatt. "You don't know who the firebug is, so you go after me." He sighed. "I'm your fall guy."

Hughes laughed. "You make it sound like the mob is after you," he said. "Well, they're not. No one is after you. All anyone wants is to catch and punish this arsonist." He collected the photographs and put them back in the file. "Right now, it looks like that's you."

"You couldn't be more wrong," said Wyatt.

Hughes nodded. "So, make it right," he said. "Tell me where you were and what you were doing when the fire was set." He leaned forward and stared into Wyatt's eyes. "Tell me something I can believe."

Wyatt stomped his right foot. "Fine. Here is what happened." Wyatt went on to describe his evening. He spoke about riding through town, coming across the empty carousel, and falling asleep on the horse. He kept his nightmare to himself. He didn't want to share that.

"I woke up on the horse," said Wyatt. "My head cleared, and I got on my bike to go home. When I got there, I saw the police cars in front of my house." He leaned forward. "You know the rest."

"Can anyone verify your story?" asked Hughes. Wyatt looked dejectedly down at his feet. "Can anyone verify your whereabouts during either of the fires?" asked Hughes. Wyatt shook his head.

"Then I'm sorry to have to do this." Hughes got up and left the room.

The police officers from Wyatt's driveway entered the room. The tall officer unlocked the suspect from the table as the shorter cop read Wyatt his legal rights. The words sent chills through Wyatt. He dropped his head and wondered how he got caught up in this mess.

****

The county jail cell was occupied by five prisoners. Wyatt sat on a bench in the musty room and leaned back against the wall. His companions included a drunk man in his sixties, a teen who brought a gun to school, and two prostitutes dressed in flimsy outfits.

Wyatt shot to his feet when he saw his brother enter the cage. The others ignored the uniformed police officer, but Wyatt rushed over to Colin. He hugged his younger brother, who hugged him back. "Man, am I glad to see you," said Wyatt. "You gotta get me out of here."

Colin put a concerned hand on Wyatt's shoulder. "It won't be easy," said Colin. He led his brother to a corner of the cell. "The judge isn't backing off his bail amount. He is trying to make an example of you."

"An example of me?" asked Wyatt. "But I didn't do anything!" he shouted. The other prisoners glanced at him. He lowered his voice. "I didn't do anything," repeated Wyatt. "Why can't he make an example of someone who is actually guilty."

"Because Sheriff Hughes is facing an election in 11 months," said Colin. "This is the biggest case of his career, and he can't stand by and do nothing as someone burns down his town," said Colin. He looked passed Wyatt to see if anyone else were listening. "He had to arrest someone to show the voters that he is still the best man for the job."

Wyatt sat down on the bench. Colin sat down beside him. "In the meantime, the real arsonist is out there, ready to burn down something else," said Wyatt. He noticed a skeptical look on Colin's face. "You know I didn't do this?" he said. "Right?"

Colin patted Wyatt's right arm. "I want to believe that Wyatt," said Colin. "I really do." He stood up and took a few steps forward. Colin turned back to face his brother. "Look, there is some compelling evidence against you."

"Like what?" asked Wyatt. "Containers of kerosene that don't have my fingerprints on them?" He shook his head. "Isn't it funny that they appeared in the garage just as the sheriff needed to arrest someone? That's some good luck for Hughes."

Colin rubbed his eyes. "I don't know what to believe at this point," he said. "But I will keep investigating the case as long as I can," he said. He moved closer to Wyatt and nearly whispered. "I just need to keep a low profile. If Hughes finds out I'm still working on your case, he will fire me."

Wyatt rose from the bench. "I'm sorry, Colin," he said. "I know you are sticking your neck out for me. I appreciate it." They shook hands and fell into a sibling hug.

"I'm going to go now," said Colin. "I am working on getting you released." He called for the guard. The gate swung open, and Colin stood by as it closed again. Colin leaned against the bars. "Hang in there, Wyatt," he said. "You will be home before you know it." He tapped the jail door with his hand as he stepped away from the cell.

Wyatt found his seat on the bench. He diverted his eyes from the others in the cell. Wyatt rested his head in his hands and waited for another nightmare to start. He drifted off, but there were no nightmares to terrorize him.

****

The smell of watermelons awakened Wyatt from a fractured sleep. He sat up and blinked his eyes multiple times until his vision was restored. He saw a female figure standing outside the jail cell with something in her hands. Wyatt slowly rose to his feet. The cell door opened, and the woman entered. She walked directly toward Wyatt.

"You look like Hell," said Kasey Carpenter. She raised the item in her hands and showed it to Wyatt. It was a mini basket fill with watermelon slices. "Colin told me that this was your favorite fruit," she added. Wyatt smiled and took the basket from her. Kasey touched his chin. "When was the last time you slept?" she asked.

Wyatt yawned and shook his head. "I don't know," he said. "What time is it?" He didn't wait for an answer. Instead, he picked up a slice and bit into it. The juicy fruit tasted like a gift from the gods. "This is terrific," he said.

"I'm glad you like it," said Kasey. She pointed to the bench and they both sat down. "It's 8:30 in the morning," she said. She wrinkled her nose. "It smells awful in here."

"Yes, it does," said Wyatt. "With all the taxes this county collects, you'd think they could afford a can of Lysol in here." He finished the first slice and took another. He tilted the basket toward Kasey. "I'm so rude," he said. "Do you want some?" he asked.

"No, I'm good," said Kasey. She folded her hands as she watched Wyatt eat. "The evidence against you is ridiculous," she said. "I can't believe that it's enough to hold you here." She glanced at the other prisoners before looking back at Wyatt. "When is your arraignment?" she asked.

"I don't know," said Wyatt. He carefully wiped some juice from his face. "I haven't even met my lawyer yet. The county is supposed to arrange one for me."

Kasey patted Wyatt on the knee. "I'll have my father call his lawyer and see if there is anything we can do to speed that up," she said. She looked around again. "Is there anything else that you need?" she asked. "Like a Tetanus shot?"

"Maybe later," replied Wyatt. He ate another slice of the watermelon and wiped his face with his shirt sleeve. "There is something I'd like you to do," he said. "Can you check in on my father?" he asked. "He hasn't been here to see me yet, and I'm worried about him."

"Sure, I'd be happy to," said Kasey. Her cell phone buzzed, and she removed it from her coat pocket. She shook her head as she read something. "This might be why your father hasn't come to see you." She handed Wyatt her phone.

Wyatt saw a news story with a photo of the front of his father's house. The headline read: *Arrest Made For Area Arsons.* "That's just great," said Wyatt. "With all those reporters there, he might not ever leave his house." He handed the phone back to Kasey.

"I'll check on him anyway," said Kasey. She put her phone back into her coat pocket. Kasey stood up. "I should get going. I don't want to stick to anything in here."

Wyatt rose to meet her. "Thank you, Kasey," he said. "For everything." He handed her the empty fruit basket. "Mostly for believing in me. There's not a lot of that going around right now." He slowly leaned toward Kasey and hugged her.

"I have a shift today, but I'll try to come back after," said Kasey.

"When this is all over," said Wyatt. "I'll take you out for a nice steak dinner," he said. Kasey smiled at him. "It's the least I can do."

"Remember, I don't date firefighters," replied Kasey. She walked a few steps away from Wyatt before turning to face him again. She shrugged. "Maybe this one time I can make an exception." She called for the guard.

The cell door opened and a man in a beige suit appeared. He carried a brown briefcase in his hand as he stepped passed Kasey, who stopped on the outside of the cell. The man walked right up to Wyatt. "Mr. James," he said. "My name is Charles Prichard." He extended a hand and Wyatt politely shook it. "I am your lawyer."

Wyatt flashed a smile at Kasey, who remained standing outside the cell. "Boy, am I glad to meet you," said Wyatt. He looked the man up and down. "That's a nice suit for civil service lawyer," he said. "They must be paying you more than I thought."

Prichard shook his head. "No, I'm not court appointed," he said. "Your father hired my firm to represent you."

"My father hired you?" asked Wyatt. Prichard shook his head. "But how can he afford you? We are not a rich family."

"He put up his home as collateral," said Prichard. He patted Wyatt's right shoulder. "Don't worry, our senior partner is friends with your father. We are barely charging him for our work. Just don't jump bail on us."

"Don't jump?" Wyatt's voice trailed off. It took a moment for him to realize that the lawyer was joking. "Oh, right," he added. "No worries there."

Prichard pointed to where Wyatt had been sitting. “Let’s sit down and discuss your release,” he said. He took Wyatt by the arm and led him back to the bench. “This won’t take long.”

Chapter Seven

Kasey hit the horn on her car. "What's the damn holdup?" she shouted. The roads were usually empty in the early afternoon, but something had this road clogged up. She listened to her scanner and did not hear about any accidents in area. She hit her horn again. "C'mon, some of us are trying to get to work!" she shouted.

The cars in her lane finally crawled ahead as Kasey kept looking for the cause of the delay. She made it around a turn and saw the problem. Dozens of people holding signs marched in front of City Hall. Some of them spilled into the street and refused to move. Two police units were on the scene with their car lights flashing.

Kasey pulled her vehicle over to the side of the road and parked it. She got out and walked toward the protesters. As she got closer to them, she read their signs. One read *Keep Firebugs in Jail*, another read *Don't Let James Burn Down Our Town*, while a different sign read *Lock Up the Arsonist!* The protesters shouted and waved their signs at Kasey as she weaved her way through the crowd toward Sheriff Hughes.

The lawman held a bullhorn in his hands. Colin James stood beside the sheriff and tried to maintain some sense of order. "Ladies and gentlemen!" said Hughes, through the bullhorn. "We understand your concern, and we respect your right to protest. But please stay off the road and limit your marching to the sidewalk."

Some in the crowd booed the sheriff. Hughes shook his head and turned off the bullhorn. He saw Kasey approaching and he quickly said something to Colin. The deputy stepped between the sheriff and the firefighter. "What are you doing here, Kasey?" asked Colin.

Kasey crossed her arms over her chest. “I’m trying to get to work,” she replied. She looked passed Colin. “How long have they been here?” she asked.

“Since word got out that my brother was released,” replied Colin. He leaned toward Kasey. “You wouldn’t have had anything to do with that getting out, would you?” he asked. Colin eyed her suspiciously.

“No, I wouldn’t,” said Kasey. “I know how to keep my mouth shut,” she added. “Not everyone on the police force can say the same,” she said. Kasey tried to step around Colin, but he cut her off. “What are you doing?” she asked.

“The sheriff is busy right now, Kasey,” he said. “Whatever you need, you can ask me.” He lowered he head slightly. His serious eyes bore into hers. “But it would be best if you got back in your car and kept on driving to work,” he said.

“Is that your idea of our two departments working together?” asked Kasey. She tried to step around him again, but he cut her off again. “Fine,” said Kasey. “Is your brother getting any police protection?” she asked.

“No,” replied Colin. A look of frustration came upon him. “There is not enough manpower to do that.” His voice softened. “I’m taking every chance I can to see him.” He looked back at his boss before turning to speak to Kasey. “Hughes doesn’t know that, and I’d rather not have him find out.”

Hughes turned on the bullhorn and he addressed the crowd again. “We know that you are frustrated, but Wyatt James has rights. His lawyer posted bail and he was legally released. We have Wyatt is under constant surveillance and he will not be able to leave town.”

Kasey leaned in closer to Colin. “Promise me that you will take care of your brother,” she said. “That you will not let this mob tear him to pieces.” She grabbed Colin’s coat and shook him. “Promise me,” she said.

Colin gently removed Kasey’s hands from his coat. “I promise I will do everything I can to help Wyatt,” he said. “Don’t grab me again. I don’t want to arrest you for assaulting a police officer.” He looked over his shoulder again at his boss, before turning back to face Kasey. “Please go to work and let me do my job.”

Kasey nodded. She pointed to a sign that one protester was waving. It read *Fire Colin Now!* “It appears that some of them are after you too,” she said. “Watch your step.”

“I always do,” said Colin. He pivoted around to face the crowd. “Back off the road!” yelled the deputy. He moved toward the protesters. “Keep off the road!” He waved his hands at the crowd to emphasize his point.

Kasey shook her head and slowly worked her way back toward her car. She got into her vehicle and carefully maneuvered it back onto the road. It took time and patience before she was able to drive past the protestors. She saw Colin as he continued to battle with the crowd. Kasey pushed a lock of hair from her eyes as she wondered if Colin would keep his promise.

****

Fire Truck One glistened under the late-afternoon sun as members of Kasey’s unit cleaned the silent behemoth. Kasey exited the fire station wearing jeans and an old Van Halen T-shirt. She removed a sponge from a bucket of soapy water and began wiping down the vehicle.

“Nice of you to join us,” said Lance, as he scrubbed the front fender. He moved away from the other men and stood beside Kasey. “I was beginning to think that you had joined the police force,” he joked. Some of the other guys laughed.

“I got caught in traffic,” she replied. She squirted the truck with water and moved to another section of the vehicle. Lance followed her. The dirt was caked on, forcing Kasey to scrub the steel surface as hard as she could. “What did you guys due to this truck?” she asked.

“We drove it through a briar patch,” said one of the other firefighters.

Kasey shook her head. “I wouldn’t doubt it.” Lance edged closer to her. Kasey elbowed him in the side. “Give me some room, Bonehead,” she joked. “Unless you want me to wash your hair for you.”

Lance smiled. “Maybe on our second date,” he said. He deliberately splashed her with water from his sponge. Kasey retaliated, and, for a moment, the mundane task turned playful as she and Lance started a water fight. The other fire fighters joined in, spraying, and splashing each other with soap and water.

The revelry died down and the workers focused on the task at hand. Lance stayed close to Kasey. “I hear you’ve been spending time with Wyatt,” said Lance. He dunked his sponge and ringed out the excess water.

“I’m just trying to help the guy,” said Kasey. “He is in a tough spot.”

“How serious are you two?” asked Lance.

"Not that it is any of your business," said Kasey. "But we are just friends." She turned away from Lance and hoped that she sounded convincing. She dunked her sponge into a bucket and started on a new section. Kasey blinked a few times to get some soap off her eyelashes.

"It's none of my business," said Lance. "But I think it's a bad idea to be around him right now," he said. "Everyone thinks he started the fires. Maybe you should keep your distance from him, at least until his trial is over."

Kasey stopped working and she glared at Lance. "I know he is innocent," she said. "He isn't the kind of person that would put people's lives in jeopardy. He is a fire fighter, not a fire starter." She picked up the bucket and moved to the other side of the truck.

Lance followed Kasey and he stood directly behind her. "No matter what you think, Wyatt James is an arson suspect," he stated. "And no matter how short-handed we are, he will never be part of this unit." Lance turned to enter the fire house, but he stopped dead in his tracks when he saw Capt. Sam Carpenter.

"Hello sir," said Lance. He paused for an awkward moment before slipping around his boss and disappearing inside the building.

"Everything alright, Kasey?" asked Sam. His daughter nodded and kept washing the truck. Sam moved closer to her. "I heard what Lance said. As wrong as it may seem, I understand his position. Most of the crew do not want Wyatt working here."

Kasey tossed her sponge into a bucket. "Then most of the crew can go to Hell!" she snapped. She tried to storm past her father, but he stood in her path. Kasey stopped at glared at her boss. "Is that how you feel about Wyatt?" she asked.

"No, it isn't," replied Sam. He gently placed a hand on Kasey's right shoulder. "I've known the James family for a long time. I watched Wyatt and Colin grow up in this town. They are both fine men with good hearts." He glanced at the other firefighters. Some had stopped working to listen to their leader. "I have no doubt that Wyatt is innocent, and that justice will prevail."

Kasey smiled at her father. "Thanks, Dad. I'm glad you feel that way."

"However," continued Sam, "I do think it would be a good idea for Wyatt to avoid our firehouse until after his name is cleared." He lifted his hand and let it fall to his side. "We don't want to bring any undue conflict to our unit." Sam stood back to allow his daughter to pass.

Kasey eased passed her father and entered the firehouse. She saw Lance sitting alone in the den with the television off. Kasey shook her head and sat down on the couch next to Lance. "You look like you just lost a basketball game to a girl," she joked. Lance remained still. Kasey shook his left shoulder. "Say something, pea brain," she said.

Lance slowly turned to face Kasey. "I'm sorry if I upset you," he said. "You know how I feel about you, and I just want what is best for you." He paused, as if searching for his words. "I can accept that you are not interested in me, but I don't want to see you get hurt by someone who obviously has mental problems."

Kasey lightly patted Lance's leg. "I appreciate your concern," she said. "Now please trust my judgement. I want to get to know Wyatt better, and from what I already know, he is not capable of deliberately starting fires." She looked up into Lance's eyes. "Maybe you should spend some time getting to know him. You'll see what I mean."

****

Fire Truck One raced through the streets of Penn Hills with its siren blasting. Kasey nervously held onto her seat as the vehicle weaved in and out of lanes en-route to its destination. The call came in from a witness to a two-car accident. There was no fire, but a woman and a child were trapped inside one of the vehicles.

The fire truck screeched to a halt and firefighters converged onto the scene. A delivery truck with severe front-end damage sat on the side of the road facing the wrong way. The vehicle in the middle of the road was the main concern. The two-door coupe lay on its side, with the driver's side door pinned against the ground.

Police officers kept curious onlookers at bay, while the firefighters tried to come up with a game plan. The captain was not onsite, which meant that Lance was in charge. Lance surveyed the coupe before shouting out orders. "Thompson, get the crane and attach it to the bumper," he said to one of the firefighters. "We are going to slowly lower the vehicle back onto all four wheels." Thompson nodded and raced back to the truck.

The unit worked together to hook up the crane and carefully lower the car. The coupe's raised tires eventually touched the ground as the car sat upright. A group of EMTs checked on the woman and her child. Lance and Kasey stood close by to keep an eye on things.

The lead EMT turned to Lance. "They are in pretty bad shape," he said. "We'll need your team to cut off the passenger-side door to get the victims out." Lance stuck his head inside the vehicle as the EMT waited for an answer. "Well, what do you think?" he asked.

Lance turned to Kasey. "Do it," he said. "Get Collins to help you."

Kasey helped fellow firefighter Jeb Collins operate the oversized power-saw as the blades cut into the crushed metal. Sparks flew everywhere as Collins carefully guided the tool over the car's frame. Three other firefighters held onto the door and pulled it away from the vehicle when Collins finished. The EMTs cautiously removed the driver and bandaged up her wounds.

Kasey peeked inside the wreckage and saw that the boy was pinned in behind the passenger front seat. He was not moving or making any sounds. Kasey turned to Lance. "I don't think he's breathing," she said. Kasey pointed to the mangled front seat. "We need to cut that away to reach him," she said.

"Get the smaller power-saws and I'll help you get him out," said Lance. He followed Kasey back to the truck. She handed him one saw, while she grabbed another. They raced back to the vehicle and started cutting away the debris. The blades sliced through the material, which Lance pushed aside to reach the boy.

Lance lifted the child and cautiously removed him from the rear of the car. He placed the child on a gurney and stepped back to let the EMTs do their work. Kasey stood next to Lance and held her breath as she watched the medical team try to revive the boy. She let out a sigh of relief when she heard the boy cry.

Two ambulances dashed off to take the injured mother and son to the hospital. Kasey and her team gathered their equipment as the crowd began to disperse. Kasey leaned against the fire truck and sipped water from a bottle. She was about to get inside the truck, when she spotted a familiar man walking toward a coffee shop. Kasey turned to Collins. "Jeb. Tell Lance I'm going to stick around for a while," she said. "I'll find a ride to the station."

The man pulled open the door to the coffee shop and stepped inside. Kasey looked at her reflection in one of the firetruck windows. She wished that she had time to cleanup, but she didn't want to waste this opportunity. She dumped a little water into her hands and wiped her face. *That will have to do*, she thought.

Kasey hustled across the street but stopped in front of the coffee shop door to compose herself. She took a breath and let it out before she opened the shop door. Her feet could barely function. She forced them to move her forward until she stopped behind a line of customers.

Kasey watched Wyatt as he patiently waited his turn. A woman standing behind Wyatt pointed at him and spoke to a man standing with her. "That's Wyatt James," she said. "He's the one who set those fires." She wrinkled her nose. "What is he doing here?" she asked.

The man next to her shrugged. "Maybe he's thirsty," he said. He waved his right hand at the woman. "Don't make a fuss. We will be out of here soon."

"I'm not making a fuss," said the woman. She drew the attention of those around her, and soon other people in line were looking at Wyatt and whispering about him.

Wyatt tried to ignore the negative attention. He finally reached the front of the line and smiled at the barista. Kasey stepped closer to hear them. "Hi, can I get a large coffee with two sugars?" he asked. He removed his wallet to pay.

The barista glared at him. She turned and walked away from the counter. That made the patrons even chattier. The barista returned with a man whose nametag identified him as the manager. "What is the problem here?" asked the manager.

Wyatt sheepishly shrugged. "No problem," he said. "I just want a large coffee."

"We don't serve criminals here, Mac," said the manager. He pointed toward the front door. "You can take your business elsewhere." The manager frowned as he held his hand outward. Wyatt didn't move. The manager lowered his arm. "So, we do have a problem then."

"You're the problem!" yelled Kasey. She stormed past the customers in front of her until she stood face-to-face with the manager. "This man risks his life to help others and all he asks for is a chance to buy a lousy cup of coffee." She thrust a finger into the man's chest. "You outta be ashamed of yourself." She turned to face the customers. "All of you should be ashamed."

The manager stepped around the counter. "That's it, lady," he said. "You're out of here." He tried to grab Kasey's right arm, but she pulled it away. "Look, I want both of you to get out of my store or I'll call the cops."

Several customers took out their cell phones and recorded the confrontation.

Kasey noticed their actions. "Good," she said to them. "Get this on video. Show the whole world how these ingrates treat a hero." She moved back toward the manager. "Wyatt James is innocent, and you are going to feel like a jackass when he clears his name."

"This guy is a firebug, and I want him gone," said the manager. He started to grab Wyatt but thought better of it when Wyatt glared at him. The manager moved to the back of the counter and pulled out his cell phone. "I'm calling the cops."

Kasey tried to lunge at the manager, but Wyatt held her back. "C'mon, let's get out of here," he said. "We can get better coffee at a diner." He put an arm around Kasey's waist and guided her out of the coffee shop. Kasey looked back one last time and saw that the manager had put his phone away without making a call.

Once outside, Kasey screamed out in frustration. "Oh, I can't stand people like that," she said. She smacked her hands together. "Small-minded morons who wouldn't recognize the truth if it bit them in the butt." She stopped talking and looked at Wyatt. "I'm sorry that happened," she said. "Penn Hills is a good place with good people." She glanced back at the coffee shop. "Or, at least I used to think so."

"Forget it," said Wyatt. He started walking away from the coffee shop and Kasey followed alongside him. "These people are just scared. They want someone to blame for the fires and right now that's me." He shook his head. "I shouldn't have gone in there. I just wanted to get out of the house and walk around for a bit. I didn't even think when I walked in there."

"You should be able to go wherever you want," said Kasey. She matched his stride as they moved along the sidewalk. "A person is supposed to be innocent until proven otherwise," she said. "I guess they forgot about that."

They walked through town in silence for several minutes. Kasey noticed the nasty looks they got from the townsfolk they encountered. She wanted to yell at each of them, but she kept quiet out of respect for Wyatt. Kasey found herself more attracted to him than ever before.

The sky darkened as they came upon a park. Wyatt sat down on a bench and Kasey sat next to him. "This was always such a nice town," said Wyatt. "I really liked growing up here." He pointed to a baseball field behind them. "Colin and I would come here nearly every day in the summer with our friends. We played baseball for hours until it got dark." He smiled slowly. "Those were the days."

Kasey nodded. "I know. My friends and I had a blast coming here," she said. "We played basketball all the time right over there," she said, pointing to the nearby court. "As we got older, we'd sneak out at night and meet here to drink beer and make out with boys."

"It's sad how quickly those days go by," said Wyatt. He shook his head. "As a kid, you look forward to the future. As an adult, you long for the past." He paused and looked around. "I know, I sound like an old man. But it's true, I really miss that time."

"We both still have a lot of life ahead of us," said Kasey.

"As long as I manage to stay out of jail," said Wyatt. He laughed. "My best chance of proving my innocence now is to have a good alibi when the arsonist strikes again." He paused and looked down at his feet. "He will, soon. Now that he thinks he won't get caught."

"The police will get him," said Kasey. "I believe that."

Wyatt looked up at Kasey. "Thank you for sticking up for me at the coffee shop," he said. "It's good to know that I have at least one friend in this town."

Kasey rested a hand on his. "You can always count on me," she said.

Wyatt slowly leaned in close to Kasey, but she pulled away from him before he could kiss her. "I need to get back to the firehouse," she said, rising to her feet. "My unit must be worried about me."

"Of course," said Wyatt. He stood up and kept a respectable distance. "Do you want me to call you an Uber or something?" he asked.

"No, I'll find my way back." She reached out and touched his arm. "I'll see you later."

Kasey walked away from Wyatt, and she fought the urge to look back at him.

Chapter Eight

After a long and restless night, Kasey rolled out of bed and stumbled into the bathroom. She turned on the light and washed her face with hot water. She took care of other things before she moved toward the kitchen. Tiger bumped against Kasey's right leg and meowed. Kasey tried to wave off the animal. "Give me a second to wake up first," she said.

The kitchen light poured down on Kasey and Tiger as they entered the room. Kasey shuffled over the cold tiles in her bare feet. She located the coffee machine and turned it on. Tiger brushed against her left leg. "I know you're hungry," said Kasey. "I'm hungry too. Let's see what we have for breakfast."

Kasey opened a cabinet and found a box of dry cat food. She dumped it into Tiger's food bowl before putting the box back. Tiger buried its head into the bowl and started eating. "There, that takes care of you," said Kasey. She took bread out of a bread box and dropped two slices into a toaster. The toasted bread popped up just as the coffee finished brewing.

The firefighter took her breakfast into her small living room. She sat on a couch and picked up the TV remote. Kasey sipped her coffee and watched the morning news. The third report caught her attention. It featured amateur video of the encounter she and Wyatt had at the coffee shop. Kasey turned up the volume.

A local TV-reporter interviewed a resident who claimed to have shot the video. "I was just standing in line waiting for a chance to order when the manager had some words with Wyatt James," said the woman. "Then some woman behind me ran up front and started arguing with the manager. It happened so fast."

Another person said she feared for her life when she realized that Wyatt was in the store. "I was truly scared," she said. "What if he were here to burn this place down with us in it?" she asked. "We wouldn't stand a chance."

The report cut back to the studio, where the anchor reminded everyone that Wyatt has not been convicted of anything. Another TV journalist appeared and introduced a legal expert, who discussed Wyatt's legal options. The expert said that Wyatt should confess.

Kasey picked up the remote and clicked off the TV. She sat back in her seat and sighed. Tiger jumped up on Kasey's lap and purred. Kasey rubbed the cat's head. "Everyone thinks he's guilty," she said. "I think he is innocent. I don't have any proof, of course, but I can't believe he would deliberately set a fire."

Tiger buried its head into Kasey's shoulder. "He tried to kiss me last night," said Kasey. She expected the cat to stop and look up at her. Instead, the feline kept rubbing its head against Kasey's shirt. "I pulled away from him, but I really wanted him to kiss me. I think," she said. She shrugged. "I don't know."

Her cell phone rang, and she quickly answered it. "Hey Dad," she said. "I know, I'm running a bit late." She sipped her coffee. "Yes, I'll be in shortly." She nodded. "Yes, Dad. I love you too."

Kasey hung up the phone and returned to her dilemma. "I really like Luke," she told the cat. "But Wyatt is so beautiful. I don't know what to do." Kasey pushed her face into a pillow and screamed. She pulled her face away and looked for Tiger. The cat stood against the far wall with its tail in the air. "Sorry, Tiger. I didn't mean to scare you." Kasey slowly rose and walked back toward the bathroom with her cat following close behind her.

****

The note on the firehouse refrigerator was addressed to Kasey. She recognized Lance's handwriting. *Check the tire pressure and oil level on Truck One.* Kasey sighed and yanked the message off the refrigerator door. She crumbled it and threw it into the trashcan.

Kasey put on plastic kitchen gloves before using the gauge to check the tires' air pressure. She added air to two tires that were low. Next, she accessed the engine and pulled out the dipstick. She wiped the stick on a clean rag before putting it back in. She withdrew the stick and was glad to see that the oil level was full. Without realizing it, Kasey wiped sweat from her forehead with the dirty glove. She replaced the dipstick and closed the engine cover.

The firefighter walked toward the back of the garage where saw Lance squatting in front of his motorcycle. Some engine parts were scattered at his feet. Kasey stopped and laughed. "What is it with firefighters and motorcycles?" she asked. "Isn't our job dangerous enough?"

Lance turned and smiled at her. "Most of us love that rush of adrenaline that you get from riding, and fighting fires," he said. Lance tossed a clean rag toward Kasey. "You have some grease on your forehead," he said.

She turned away in embarrassment and quickly cleaned her face. "Thanks," she said. "It would have taken me a while to realize that on my own." Kasey put the rag on nearby table. "That's all I would need. Having the guys see me that way. I'd never hear the end of it."

"I don't know," said Lance. "I think you look cute with a little grease on you." He laughed. "And I've seen you drive. You like to go fast too."

Kasey shrugged. "Maybe a little."

"Dating can be dangerous too," added Lance. "Especially when you are dating an arson suspect." He walked over to a min-refrigerator and took out two bottles of water. He handed one to Kasey. "I saw the video on the news."

"Who hasn't?" asked Kasey. "But we are not dating. Wyatt and I are just friends." She opened the water bottle and drank the cool liquid. She removed her dirty gloves before wiping her mouth.

"I've seen the way he looks at you, Kasey," said Lance. He nodded. "And the way you look at him. You both want more than friendship." He kneeled in front of his motorcycle and continued with the repairs. "I remember that you used to date firefighters. Like Nick Shaumback." He glanced at Kasey. "You two were quite an item."

"That was a long time ago," said Kasey. She squeezed the bottle and some water spilled out. "It's all in the past now." She stepped away from Lance before turning around to face him. "I won't do that again."

Lance put down his tools and rose to his feet. "It wasn't your fault that Nick got hurt in that fire," he said. "No one blames you. It could have happened to any one of us."

Kasey's eyes welled up. "No one blames me for it, but everyone knows that I screwed up," she said. She stared down at her feet for a moment. "I didn't stay close to him, and I got lost. He came back to find me, and that damn frame collapsed."

"You were only on the job for a few months," said Lance. "Nick was a five-year veteran. He was responsible for you, not the other way around."

"It doesn't matter," said Kasey. "Seeing him lying there in that hospital bed with tubes sticking out of him, not knowing if he were going to survive." She shook her head. "That was too much for me. I will never put myself or anyone else through that again."

Lance slowly moved toward Kasey. He gently wrapped his arms around her. "I'm sorry I brought all that up," he said. "I didn't mean to upset you." He kissed her left cheek.

Kasey pulled away from Lance. She wiped her eyes again. "I've got to get lunch ready for the guys," she said. She marched into the firehouse and closed the door behind her. Kasey stopped and clenched her fists. She tried to pull herself together before any of her crew saw her.

****

The arson investigator's report was twenty pages long, a succinct account of three arson fires in Penn Hills, Pa.

Kasey put the report down and rubbed her tired eyes. Capt. Sam Carpenter sat patiently across from her in the firehouse living room. Kasey looked over at her father. The squad leader's expressionless face was the reason he won so many poker games.

"Kerosene was the cause of all three fires," recapped Sam. "No doubt about it. I'm sorry to say that doesn't bode well for Wyatt James."

"It doesn't prove his guilty," said Kasey. "It doesn't prove anything."

"The timing of the fires and the kerosene in the James home look bad for Wyatt," said Sam. "You know that most people already believe he is guilty. This will only confirm their suspicions."

"So, what do we do now?" asked Kasey.

Sam reached over and placed a hand on his daughter's arm. "I'm don't know if there is anything we can do to help him." He lifted his hand and sat back in his seat. "I know how you feel about him. I like him too. But this might not end the way you want it to."

"We should look at the locations of the fires to see if there is any pattern," said Kasey. "Maybe we can figure out the perp's hunting ground and zero in on where he lives."

"The investigators already tried that," said Sam. "They didn't find any discernable pattern to the fires." He shook his head. "It's like the arsonist is picking places at random."

"We should check again," said Kasey. She knew that she sounded frantic, but she couldn't stand doing nothing.

Sam stood up and moved around the room. "The fires were at St. Mary's Church, Warner's Import Warehouse, and Tony's Grocery," he said. "The report noted that they have different owners, they are in different neighborhoods, and none of them were in financial trouble." He sat down again across from Kasey. "No discernable pattern," he repeated.

Kasey rubbed her eyes again. "He has to be using some criteria to pick his targets."

"Now you are thinking logically," said Sam. "By doing so, you are eliminating one very important possible factor."

"What's that?" asked Kasey. She leaned forward in anticipation.

"The arsonist might be crazy," said Sam. Kasey shook her head. "I don't mean to be politically incorrect," said Sam. "But a lack of pattern could be a clue itself. Maybe the perp is mentally unstable. He could be hearing voices in his head or something."

Kasey snapped her fingers and stood up. "That's not a bad idea, Dad," she said. She pulled her cellphone out of her pocket and dialed a number. "Sheriff Hughes, please," she said. Kasey looked at a clock above the television. "Oh, sorry, I didn't realize how late it was. Can I leave him a message?"

Sam stretched his hands over his head. "He's probably in bed already," he said.

"Yes, this is Kasey Carpenter. He knows who I am," said Kasey. "It's about the arson case. Ask him to please check to see if there were any recently released inmates from mental hospitals in the area," she said. "What? No really. That could help the investigation. Okay, thank you." She hung up and turned to face her father.

"You know he's never getting that message," said Sam. He rose and moved toward the kitchen. "The answering service must be getting all kinds of crackpot calls and they'll think yours is one of them."

Kasey followed Sam and watched him pour coffee into a clean cup. He glanced back at his daughter. "Do you want some?" he asked. She shook her head. "Look, it's not a bad idea. I'll talk to Hughes in the morning." He drank some coffee as Kasey yawned. "You should go home and get some sleep," said Sam. "It is very late."

"You're right," she said. She approached her father and gave him a quick hug. "Good night, Dad. I'll talk to you tomorrow."

"Good night, sweetie," replied Sam. He kissed her on the forehead.

Kasey turned off the lights in the living room and kitchen before she exited the firehouse. She locked the front door and turned on the flashlight on her cell phone. The beam cut through the darkness and shone on her car. She was a few strides away from the vehicle when she heard something rustling in the bushes to her right. Kasey turned the flashlight toward the sound, expecting to find a deer or some other animal. She froze when she saw the figure of a person.

"Hey, you!" she yelled. She kept the light on the stranger. "What are you doing here?" she asked. The figure wore a black sweatshirt and black pants. A ski mask covered the face. The intruder had plastic jugs in both hands.

The stranger took off running, away from the firehouse. Kasey saw the jugs drop onto the ground as she chased the person. "Stop!" she yelled, but the stranger kept on running. Kasey pulled her phone up to her face and dialed 911.

"Nine one one, what is your emergency?" asked a voice on the phone.

"This is Kasey Carpenter at the Penn Hills Fire House," she said, breathlessly. "There is a prowler outside the station. I'm chasing him. Send me some backup."

"You're chasing him?" asked the operator.

"Yes, I am," said Kasey, as she pushed through some brush. "And it would be a lot easier if I didn't have to talk on my phone."

"Understood," said the operator. "I'm sending patrol cars to your location."

Kasey kept the line open as she tried to keep up with the stranger. The darkness made it difficult to maneuver, and she didn't see the tree root in front of her. She tripped over the root and crashed onto the hard ground. "Dammit!" she yelled, as her cell phone slipped away from her. Kasey heard the strangers' footsteps fade away.

She scrambled to her feet and scooped up her cell phone. “Are you still there?” she asked the operator. Kasey wiped mud from her face. She fought to catch her breath.

“I am still here,” said the operator. “What is going on?” she asked.

“I tripped,” admitted Kasey. “The intruder got away.”

“Do you need medical assistance?” asked the operator.

Kasey touched her neck, chest, midsection, knees, and ankles. “No, I’m fine,” she said. She heard a police siren. “It sounds like a police car is here,” she said. “Hold on.” She turned and jogged back to the firehouse.

Sheriff Hughes exited his vehicle. The lights flashed but the siren was off. “Are you hurt?” he asked Kasey. She shook her head and ended her phone call. “What’s this about a prowler?” asked Hughes.

Kasey recapped what happened as her father and other firefighters poured out of the firehouse. “He disappeared in the woods back there,” said Kasey. She pointed toward the back of the firehouse. “I might have caught him if I hadn’t tripped.”

“What were you thinking?” asked Sam. He hugged his daughter. “That guy might have had a gun. You could have been killed.” He pulled back and looked her in the eyes. “I’m glad you’re alright.”

“Thanks, Dad,” she said. She turned toward the sheriff. “I saw where he dropped the containers.” She started walked away from the group. “C’mon, they are this way.”

"Hold it!" shouted Hughes. "I don't want everyone trampling over the crime scene." He spoke into his mobile radio. "Colin, this is Hughes. Are you on your way?" he asked. There was no reply. "Colin, its Sheriff Hughes. Please respond."

There was static for a moment. "Sheriff, this is Colin," said the deputy. "I'm on my way to the firehouse. Be there shortly."

"Copy that," said Hughes. He addressed the group. "I know you are all eager to help, but the best thing you can do is go back inside. Let me and Colin investigate the scene." The firefighters turned and reentered the building. "Kasey, you and your dad can stay."

Another patrol car arrived a few minutes later. It stopped near the sheriff's vehicle. Colin got out of the car and raced over toward Hughes. The sheriff scolded him. "Where have you been, deputy?" he asked.

Colin gave a sheepish smile. "I was off-duty, Boss," he said. He glanced at Kasey before continuing. "And I wasn't alone."

Kasey smiled. "Good for you, Colin," she said.

Hughes filled Colin in on the details, before speaking to Kasey. "Will you please show us where the suspect dropped the containers?" he asked. He nodded toward the woods.

Kasey led her father and the police officers to the abandoned containers. The lawmen used their flashlights to examine them. Hughes bent down with gloves on and unscrewed the cap on one. He sniffed the contents and nodded. "Smells like kerosene," he said. He looked at Colin. "Bag these and take them to the station. Dust them for prints."

Colin followed the sheriff's orders and carried the containers to his vehicle. He drove away with his police lights on.

Hughes looked around the area but did not find any other tangible evidence. "I'll have a crime scene team come over in the morning," he said. He glanced at the sky. "It's not supposed to rain tonight. Maybe they will find something in the daylight."

The trio walked back to the firehouse. Hughes stood in front of his vehicle for a moment. He spoke into his radio. "Calvin, this is Sheriff Hughes," he said. Officer Calvin responded. "Have you had eyes on Wyatt James tonight?" he asked.

"All night," said Calvin. "He hasn't left his home since he got here this afternoon."

"Copy that," said Hughes. He took a deep breath and looked over at Kasey. "That means it wasn't Wyatt that you saw earlier," said Hughes.

"I guess not," said Kasey.

Hughes shook his head. "That also means that we are back to square one."

Chapter Nine

The movie didn't hold Wyatt's attention. He had thought that a comedy would help cheer him up, but the jokes were flat, and the plot was nonsensical. Wyatt turned it off halfway through and rested on the couch. His mind raced with questions about the arson case. *Who was really behind it? How were they able to get away with it? What was their next target? Why had they decided to frame me?* he wondered.

He sat up and rubbed his tired eyes. His future was unbearably murky. *Even if I don't go to jail*, he wondered. *What will I do with my life? I can't leave here with Dad forever.* Wyatt picked up a mug and he sipped tepid coffee. He grimaced as he rose to his feet. Bad coffee was surely not the answer.

Wyatt walked into the kitchen. He dumped the cold liquid into the sink before making himself a new cup of coffee. He leaned against the counter and watched the machine brew his drink. "I'm 29 years old," he said out loud. "I'm too young and too poor to retire. I can't go back to fighting fires. Not after what happened." He retrieved his cup from the coffee maker. "Am I too old to go back to school?" He sipped his coffee and shook his head. "I never liked school. Too many rules." He threw his left hand up into the air. "What am I going to do?" he asked.

Wyatt finished his drink in silence. He put the cup into the sink and strolled back into the living room. The television was still on, but the volume was muted. He sat back down on the couch and tried to consider his options. The lumber yard was always hiring, but that was backbreaking work for a small salary. He could apply for a government job, but the thought of sitting behind a desk for eight hours a day was truly depressing.

Wyatt picked up the TV remote and flipped through the stations with the volume still down. He half-heartedly checked out his programming options. He didn't know what he wanted to watch, but he was sure that nothing he had seen so far would hold his attention. A knock on the door brought him out of his trance.

He slowly stood up and made his way to the front door. His eyes opened wider when he saw Sheriff Hughes standing in front of Kasey and Sam Carpenter. "Good evening, Wyatt," said Hughes. "We'd like to talk to you. May we come in?"

"Sure, come on in," he said. "We need to keep it down. My dad is in bed already." He held the door until all three were inside. "The living room is this way," he added. He led his guests to the room. "Make yourself comfortable," he said, pointing to the seats. "Can I get anyone anything to drink?" he asked.

They all said no. Hughes sat on the couch where Wyatt had been sitting. "My officer outside said you've been here for hours," said the sheriff. "You didn't sneak out the back or anything?" he asked.

"No, sheriff," replied Wyatt. "I've been home the whole time." He sat down in an uncomfortable chair that was pressed against the far wall from the couch. He glanced at Kasey and her father, both of whom seemed ill at ease. "What's going on here?" he asked.

Kasey cleared her throat. "Someone tried to burn down the firehouse tonight," she said.

Wyatt shot to his feet. "What?" he asked. "Is everyone okay?"

“Yes, I chased him away before he could do any damage,” said Kasey. She blinked her eyes a few times. “I got a brief look at the suspect, but he was wearing a mask. He dropped two containers as he got away. They had kerosene in them.”

Wyatt looked over at Hughes. “Then you know I’m innocent,” he said. “You’re going to drop the charges against me?” he asked. Hughes didn’t respond. “What the Hell is wrong with you, sheriff?” asked Wyatt. “What is it going to take for you to realize that you’ve got the wrong guy? Or don’t you care about the truth?”

Hughes rose to his feet. “Don’t you dare question my integrity!” he yelled. He stood a few inches away from Wyatt. “I’ve been serving this community since you were in diapers. And just because you weren’t there tonight, doesn’t mean you’re innocent.”

Sam stood and positioned himself between Wyatt and Hughes. “Let’s all just calm down before we say or do anything we’ll regret later.” He moved closer to Hughes. “Blake, you had flimsy evidence against Wyatt to start with. The emergence of another suspect places great doubt on Wyatt being the arsonist.” He paused. “Even you have to admit that.”

“He could have a partner,” said Hughes. Wyatt turned away from him in disgust. “Or maybe it was a copy-cat looking for fame. Either way, Wyatt James is the prime suspect in this case and that’s not going to change.”

“You’re not dropping the charges?” asked Kasey. Hughes shook his head. “You are a stubborn old bastard!” she yelled. “And your arrogance might get someone killed.”

“I don’t need this,” said Hughes. He turned and walked toward the front door. He yelled over his shoulder. “You’re still under surveillance Wyatt, so don’t get any ideas about leaving town.” The lawmen exited and slammed the door behind him.

Sam turned toward Wyatt. “I’m sorry you’re getting railroaded like this,” he said. “It’s not fair, and it doesn't help us catch the real firebug.” He offered his right hand to Wyatt, who politely shook it. “I’m going to keep working on Hughes,” said Sam. “Maybe I’ll be able to convince him that he’s making a mistake.” Sam looked over at Kasey. “C’mon honey, we’ll take an Uber back to the station.”

Kasey put up her right hand. “That’s alright, Dad,” she responded. “You go, but I’m going to hang out with Wyatt for a little while. I think he needs someone to talk to.” She walked over and kissed her father on the cheek. “I’ll call you later.”

Sam glanced at Wyatt before nodding at Kasey. “Be careful getting home,” he said.

“I will, Dad,” she said. “I promise.” She patted Sam on the back, and he quietly left through the front door.

Kasey nervously cleared her throat. “Is it okay if I stay for a bit?” she asked.

Wyatt smiled. “Yes, I’d like that.” He pointed again to the chairs. “Please, have a seat. Are you hungry?” he asked. “We can order something.”

Kasey sat down and nodded. “I could go for some pizza,” she said. “Plain or pepperoni would be good.” She folded her hands in her lap. “And some cold soda.”

Wyatt picked up his cell phone and ordered their dinner from a pizza place. He hung up and sat down near his guest. “It will be here in about 40 minutes,” he said. He suddenly felt thirsty. “I’m going to get a bottled water. Would you like one?”

“Yeah, that’d be great,” she said.

Wyatt rose and left the room for a moment. He returned with two cold bottles of water. "Here you go," he said, handing one to Kasey. She opened it and took a sip. Wyatt sat beside her again. "I want to thank you again for believing in me. You and Colin and your father are about the only ones in town who think I'm innocent."

"I think more people will realize the truth soon," said Kasey. She drank more water. "Once they hear about the attempt on the firehouse while you were under police observation, they will have to admit that you are not responsible."

Wyatt smiled. "Good, then they can stop staring at me and talking about me," he said. He shook his head. "I just want to be left alone to live my life." He looked at Kasey. "Well, I'm glad you are in my corner." He reached over and touched her right hand. She didn't pull away.

"Can I ask you something personal?" asked Wyatt. Kasey nodded. Wyatt looked down at their entangled hands. "How is it that you are not married?" he asked.

Kasey curled her fingers over his. "I don't know," she answered. "I guess the right guy hasn't asked me yet." She snuggled close to him. "Why aren't you married?" she asked.

"Same thing," he replied. "I haven't met the right guy yet."

Kasey sat up and with wide eyes. "What?" she asked. She let go of his hand.

"Relax," said Wyatt. He laughed. "I was just trying to be funny."

Kasey eyed him suspiciously. "That didn't go over well," she said.

"Sorry," replied Wyatt. He inched away from Kasey to give her some space. "No, I have not met the right woman. But I am open to. I just haven't come close yet. How about you? Have you come close before?" he asked. He drank more water.

Kasey glanced at the floor for a moment. Her face lost some of its color. "I was dating a guy that I thought I would marry," she said. She looked at Wyatt. "He was a firefighter in my unit. Nick Shaumback. He was tall, smart, assertive, and kind. He was perfect."

"What happened?" asked Wyatt.

Kasey sat back against the couch. "He nearly died in a fire." She paused as her eyes moistened. "It was my fault. I made a mistake and it almost cost him everything. Afterward, we tried to make our relationship work, but my guilt got in the way. He moved to Florida, and I stayed here." Her eyes filled with tears, and she stood up to avoid looking at Wyatt.

"I'm sorry," said Wyatt. He slowly rose to his feet and moved closer to Kasey. "I didn't mean to upset you. I shouldn't have asked about that."

Kasey turned and fell into his arms. He held her without speaking. Her story made him think of Duane Wright's death. He pushed those thoughts out of his mind.

Wyatt eased back and looked into Kasey's eyes. He wiped some tears from her face. "Maybe we should sit down," he said. Kasey nodded. Wyatt led her back to her seat, and he sat beside her again.

Kasey leaned toward the television. "They're reporting on the arson case. Where is your remote?" she asked.

Wyatt lifted the remote and turned up the volume. A female reporter stood in front of Penn Hills's main courthouse. "This could be the break that Wyatt James has been looking for," said the reporter. "With a new suspect emerging while he was under observation, there has to be new doubt about his involvement in the previous fires. Police have so far not commented on this breaking development, but one source, who asked to remain anonymous, said this failed attempt on the firehouse will shift the focus of their investigation."

Wyatt muted the television. He sat back and let out a long sigh. All his muscles relaxed at once and he nearly fell off the couch. He shook his head in relief.

"Are you alright?" asked Kasey. She put a hand on his left shoulder. "You look like you are about to pass out." She kept her hand on Wyatt to steady him. "Do you want some water?"

"No, I'm good," said Wyatt. He took another deep breath. "It's just good to hear someone on TV say that I'm innocent. I've had enough of reporters trying to railroad me." He stood and paced the room for a moment. "They were still camped out here today, until the cops watching me told them to leave. I hope they finally leave me alone for good."

A knock on the door made Wyatt grimace. He walked to the front door with Kasey behind him. Wyatt laughed when he saw the pizza delivery boy. He paid for the food and carried the box to the living room. "I forgot we ordered food," he said. "I'll get some plates."

Wyatt returned from the kitchen with two plates, and he handed one to Kasey. She had already set up two folding tables, both with drinks. They sat down and starting eating. "Oh, this is so good," said Kasey. "Where did you order it from?"

Before Wyatt could answer, Kasey's cell phone rang. She took it out of her pocket. "It's work," she said. "This is Kasey," she told the caller. Kasey nodded and stood back up. "I'm on my way," she said.

Wyatt put his slice down. "What's going on?" he asked. He rose to his feet.

"There's a fire in a residential home," she said. "I've got to go." She rushed toward the front door and Wyatt followed her. She stopped at the door and looked at Wyatt. "Two of my guys are sick," she said. "We are more shorthanded than ever. Can you help us?" she asked.

Wyatt swallowed hard. His hands began to shake. "No," he said, barely getting the word out. He turned away in embarrassment.

Kasey touched his right arm. "I understand, Wyatt," she said. She leaned toward him and kissed him on the cheek. "I'll see you soon." She turned and hurried out the door.

Wyatt closed the front door and stood motionless.

He forced himself to return to the living room. He picked up his half-eaten slice of pizza, but suddenly found that he had no appetite. Wyatt boxed up the food and put it into the refrigerator. He suddenly felt the urge to flee.

Wyatt left the kitchen and moved swiftly toward the garage. He opened the garage door and pushed his motorcycle onto the driveway. He closed the garage door and started up the motorcycle. He revved the engine a few times, feeling the vibrations through his body. Wyatt put the bike into gear and sped out into the night.

He didn't have a destination in mind. Wyatt rode through the streets of Penn Hills, opening up the bike and going faster than he should have. An odd sense of dread filled him, even as he knew that he had been exonerated by the press. He felt the need to go faster, so he twisted the throttle and shifted gears. The streetlights became a blur and the bike started shaking. Even with his heart pounding, Wyatt did not want to slow down. He leaned into the hard turns and yanked the bike back as it nearly tumbled over.

Wyatt rode the bike like it were a run-away bull. Sweat rolled down his face and stung his eyes. He spit to the side to empty his mouth. His head began to ache. He nearly spilled when the bike bounced over a rough spot on the road that would have sent him skidding along the asphalt. Wyatt finally slowed and downshifted, until he regained full control of the machine.

Wyatt found himself in a residential area after gliding around a turn. Up ahead were flashing red and blue lights. Wyatt stopped his bike on a curb behind a fire department barrier. He removed his helmet and watched the crew from the Penn Hills fire department battle a blaze in a two-story family home.

The images brought back memories of his last fire. He could see the thick smoke that had blinded him before, and he could hear the roof collapsing. His partner lay on the floor, with Wyatt unable to help him. He tried to shout out for help, but he could not make a sound.

A scream from a crying baby brought him back to reality. He saw residents in their sleepwear helplessly watching their homes burn. What began as a single-home fire had spread to two other homes. More firetrucks arrived from a nearby county to help combat the blaze. Firefighters from those trucks rushed toward the inferno with hoses in their hands.

Wyatt spotted Kasey as she and Lance exited one of the homes. Lance held a small child in his hands. He brought the child to an ambulance, where an EMT began treating the victim. Wyatt felt his chest tighten as Kasey rushed back inside one of the homes.

Time stood still for Wyatt as he kept a sharp eye out for Kasey. The fire consumed most of the house that she had run back into. Other firefighters came out of that house, but there was no sign of Kasey. Wyatt pressed his hands together and said a silent prayer for her.

Finally, Kasey re-emerged from the burning home. Wyatt nearly fell to his knees in relief. He felt something stir in his stomach and he quickly turned away from the scene. He stumbled a few feet and vomited between two parked vehicles.

Wyatt cleaned himself up as best he could. He returned to where he had been standing. One house was free of the destructive flames, while another collapsed to the ground. The firefighters eventually put out the remaining flareups and began their cleanup.

The crowd drifted away from the spectacle, as most people returned to their unaffected homes. Wyatt slowly rode over to the barrier behind Fire Truck One. He turned off his engine and waved his hand at Kasey. She spotted him and ran over to see him. "What are you doing here?" she asked.

"I was riding around when I saw the fires," said Wyatt. He held his helmet in his hands. "I guessed this was where you went." He peeked behind her. "Was anyone hurt?" he asked.

"Thankfully, no," said Kasey. "Everyone got out." She turned around to survey the damage. "The one house is totally destroyed," she added. Kasey shook her head. "That family lost everything in their home."

Wyatt leaned toward her and tried not to yell. "Does it look like arson?" he asked.

Kasey rubbed her chin. "No, this looks like an accident. Maybe faulty wiring somewhere. That's my guess." She stretched her arms over her head. "I think there is still a part of you that wants to fight fires. That's why you're really here."

Wyatt shook his head. "I don't think so," he replied. "When I saw you run into that home, all I could do was pray that you'd come out okay," he admitted. "My hands are still shaking."

Kasey smiled. “You prayed for me?” she asked. Wyatt nodded. “That’s the sweetest thing I’ve ever heard.” She reached out and covered Wyatt’s right hand with hers. She gave it a gentle squeeze. “Still, I think you should consider joining my squad. We need someone like you.” She paused. “And I think it’s time for you to get back in the game.”

“I don’t know if I’ll ever have the courage to do this again,” said Wyatt. He let go of her hand. “Your squad doesn’t need a member who is afraid to do the job.”

“I believe in you, Wyatt,” said Kasey. “It might take time, but you’ll get there.” She lightly punched his right arm. “We have an open house for the public in two days. Come by, meet the team. It will help you feel better.”

“I’ll think about it,” said Wyatt. “No promises.”

“I’ll see you there,” said Kasey. She leaned toward Wyatt and kissed him. Kasey’s right hand touched his cheek as they held the kiss. Kasey pulled back. “I still have work to do. I’ll see you later.”

Wyatt watched her return to her duties. He wondered how she could have so much faith in him when he didn’t have any at all in himself. He looked at the burned-out homes. Part of him did want to get back to work, but he didn’t know if he could bring himself to rush into a burning building again. *What kind of a firefighter would I be?* he wondered.

Chapter Ten

The line outside of *Harold's* poured into the parking lot. Hungry patrons stood in the light drizzle waiting for a chance to be seated. Wyatt and Colin edged their way into the dining area with their father, David. "There are too many people here," said David. "I want to go somewhere else."

"There is nowhere else to go, Dad," said Colin. "This is the best place to eat in the state, and you know it." Colin tried to get the attention of the hostess, but she walked right by him. He turned to face his brother. "Wyatt, you're the famous one, see what you can do."

Wyatt noticed a mix of friendly and unfriendly glances from some of the patrons. "I don't think I'll be much help," said Wyatt. "Half of these folks look like they want to beat me up." He nodded at a little boy in a blue coat. The boy smiled at Wyatt, but the boy's mother noticed, and she glared at Wyatt. He turned away from her. "Yes, I'm sensing a lot of hostility."

The James family stood waiting for another twenty minutes before the hostess approached them. She led the men to a four-top table in the rear of the diner. The men looked over their menus and put their orders in as soon as their waitress arrived. The apron-clad woman darted toward the kitchen with their orders.

"Wyatt, how does it feel to be a free man?" asked Colin. He picked up a straw, tapped the edge against the table, and blew the paper at Wyatt's head. Wyatt tried to retaliate, but he missed. Colin laughed and shoved Wyatt's shoulder. Wyatt shoved him back.

"Can't you two behave like grown men?" snapped David. His face reddened. "For God's sake, we are out in public." He glared at Colin. "And you represent the law in this town."

Colin and Wyatt apologized in unison. When David turned away, Wyatt punched Colin's right arm. Colin's left hand formed a fist, but he held back from hitting his brother. They stared each other down for a moment, and the horseplay ended.

David took out his cell phone. "We were in line for 32 minutes," he reported. He put his cell phone down on the table. "It will probably take that long for our food to arrive." He picked up a water glass and sloppily sipped from it. He grimaced at the other eaters. "Why are all these damn people here, anyway," he asked. "Don't they have lives?"

"It's Saturday morning, Dad," said Wyatt. "They are probably going shopping afterwards. People need to fuel up before they hit the stores." Wyatt sifted through the crowd, hoping to find Kasey in the diner. She was not there.

"How's that arson investigation going, Colin?" asked David. The question startled Colin. The lawman glanced at Wyatt without speaking. "Have you found the jerk responsible yet?" asked David. "Or do you donut-eaters still think my boy Wyatt did it?" he asked.

Colin cleared his throat and moved closer to David. "We don't think Wyatt is a viable suspect anymore," said Colin. He looked around before continuing. "We do have some solid leads though. We'll crack this case before long."

"Good," said David. He ran his fingers along his water glass. "I've lived in this community for a long time now," he said. "People are scared. More scared than I've ever seen them. You guys need to find this perp fast."

"We are doing our best, Dad," said Colin. "Just like you told us as kids: It's better to work together than apart." He nodded toward Wyatt. "We are combining the resources of the fire department and the police department to catch this firebug."

“Glad to hear it,” said David. He drank more water. “So far, you’re doing a bang-up job. Who is your next suspect? The mayor?” he asked. David fidgeted in his seat. “Why do they make this chairs so uncomfortable?” he complained.

Colin and Wyatt glanced at each other and shook their heads. “Hey Dad,” said Colin. “The Eagles’ draft choices look good this year, don’t you think?” he said. He rubbed his hands enthusiastically. “This could be our year to return to the Super Bowl.”

David shook his head. “Not with this meathead coach,” he replied. “They’ll be lucky to win 6 games, if any.” He sighed as his eyes fell on his sons. “And these players today. They don’t care about winning. For them it’s all about money.”

Wyatt goaded his father. “Not like when you were young, right Pop?” he asked. Wyatt winked at Colin. “Back in the day, the game was played by men who loved the game. They would have played for nothing.”

“Damn right,” said David. “They were better men then. They didn’t hold out for a few dollars more. They didn’t complain about the playing conditions. Those guys played for the simple joy of competing. They loved the game.”

“I think you are too hard on today’s players, David,” said a voice from behind their table. All three men turned to see who had spoken. A thin woman in her early forties smiled at the James men. “Then again, you never had patience for Humanity.” The woman paused and nodded at Wyatt and Colin. “Hello boys,” she said.

“Hello, Ms. Harvest,” said Wyatt. He had the good sense to rise and shake her hand. Colin did not stand up. “How are the fifth-graders doing this year?” he asked.

"Just as monstrous as the kids from last year," said Ms. Harvest. "With those cell phones glued to her hands, they don't even pay attention in class anymore." She edged closer to David. "David, I am deeply sorry for the loss of your wife. She was a fine woman."

David forced a smile. "Thank you, Mildred," he replied. "I appreciate that." He pointed to an empty chair at their table. "Would you care to join us?" he asked. "There is plenty of room." He shuffled to his feet to pull out the empty chair.

"Thank you, David," she replied. She sat down across from David, who quickly returned to his seat. "That was a lovely ceremony for her," said Ms. Harvest. "The flowers and the music. Just lovely," she repeated.

None of the James men knew what to say. Instead, they flashed awkward glances at each other.

"Wyatt," said the teacher. "I'm happy to hear that you are not a suspect in the arson case anymore," she added. She rested her right hand on his left arm for a moment. "I never thought you could do something like that. It's not in your nature."

"Thank you, Ms. Harvest," said Wyatt. "We ordered food," he said. "Would you like something to eat?" he asked. He pointed his left thumb at Colin. "Don't worry, he's paying for it." Wyatt elbowed Colin in the side, but the lawman refused to react.

"Yes, that would be nice," said Ms. Harvest. "I am a bit hungry, but I can pay my own way." She waved her left hand, and a waitress came over to their table. Ms. Harvest asked for an egg platter with toast, coffee, and a small cup of fruit. The waitress nodded and took off for the kitchen.

"Wyatt, how long do you plan to stay in town?" asked Ms. Harvest. She folded her hands and rested them on the table. The teacher sat straight up and looked the others in the eyes when she talked to them. Her voice ringed with authority.

Wyatt thought about his answer before he responded. "It's kind of up in the air right now," he said. He glanced at his father before looking back at the teacher. "I had planned just to stay for the funeral, but now I think I might hang around a bit longer."

"Forgive my intrusion," said Ms. Harvest. "I asked because my niece is visiting from Pittsburgh this week. She's not happy in the Steel City. She wants to relocate here, and I thought you might want to meet her. If you have time."

The waitress brought their food over to the table before Wyatt could answer. The plates were sorted out and the waitress asked if anyone needed anything else. The patrons all said that they were fine. Wyatt picked up his glass of water and he took a long drink.

"Ms. Harvest," said Colin. "I want to thank you for the flowers that you sent for my mother's service," he said. "They were beautiful. I'm sure my mother would have loved them." He raised his glass to toast their guest.

"How very kind of you, Colin," said Ms. Harvest. She smiled. "I was hoping they were not too ostentatious." She turned toward David. "I didn't want to take any attention away from your lovely wife," she said. "She will be dearly missed."

David grumbled something and took a sip of his water. Everyone ate in silence for a few minutes. The clanging of utensils added to the tension. "How is your food, Ms. Harvest?" asked Colin. "Mine is delicious."

"So is mine, dear," replied Ms. Harvest. She daintily blotted her lips with her napkin. "Tell me Colin, how is the police investigation into those terrible fires?" she asked. "Now that your brother has been cleared, who do you think might have done it?" she asked.

Colin nearly chocked on his food. He forced a smile. "I can't say too much about an ongoing investigation," he said. "But we do have some promising leads."

Ms. Harvest put her fork down on her plate. "I think you should investigate the Tolbert brothers," she said. She shook her head. "Those boys have been trouble for this town for far too long. It would be just like them to do this."

Colin nodded. "That is an interesting thought, Ms. Harvest," he said. "I will pass that along to the sheriff. I'm sure he will want to pay a call on them on their farm." He sipped some coffee. "We should have you and your niece over for dinner some night." He looked at David. "Wouldn't that be nice, Dad?" he asked.

David looked like he was put on the spot. "Yes, Ms. Harvest," he replied. "We would enjoy having you over." He ripped off a square of paper from one of the menus, and he took a pen out of his pocket. David jotted down a phone number before he handed the paper to Ms. Harvest. "Here," he said. "This is our home phone number. Call me and we'll set it up."

Ms. Harvest took the paper and put it into her pants pocket. "Thank you, David," she said. "I'm looking forward to it." She smiled at him and his sons. She was nearly finished her food when her cell phone rang. "Excuse me," she said, as she stood up. "I need to take this call." She moved away from the table as she spoke to the caller.

Wyatt watched Ms. Harvest quickly move toward the exit. “I guess she’s not coming back,” he said. He looked at Colin. “I hope that was important because she just stuck you with the bill.” He tossed a crumbled napkin at his Colin, but, again, his brother did not retaliate.

“I’ll send her a bill,” said Colin. He lifted the crumpled napkin and pretended to throw it at Wyatt, before dropping it back onto the table. “I know where she lives.”

“You will do no such thing,” said David. “We can afford to pay for her meal.”

“Relax, Dad,” said Colin. “That was just a joke.”

“Why is everything a joke to you two?” he asked. His hands tightened into fists. “Can’t you take anything seriously? Your mother just died and you both act like everything is normal!” he yelled. David pounded on the table. “What is wrong with you?”

“Dad, take it easy,” said Colin. He glanced passed his father. “You are making a scene.”

“I don’t give a damn!” shouted David. He suddenly calmed and looked at his sons. “Your mother meant the world to me. I can’t believe she’s gone.” He picked up a clean napkin and wiped his eyes. “I don’t know what I’m going to do without her. We had been together for so long that I can’t even remember what life was like before I met her.”

Wyatt reached over and touched his father’s right hand. “Dad, we’re sorry,” he said. “We are not taking her loss lightly. It’s just that we use humor to cope with pain.” He glanced at Colin. “That’s the way Colin and I have always done it. But that doesn’t mean that we aren’t in pain. I know we both are.”

“He’s right, Dad,” said Colin. “But we should have been more sensitive toward you.”

"Dad, maybe we should look into some kind of grief counseling for all of us," said Wyatt. "It would be good to unload about how we feel." He paused and tried to read his father's face. All he saw was sadness. "What you say, Dad?" he asked.

David's chin shook. "I don't need to talk to strangers about how I feel," he said. "I know how I feel." He shook his head. "If you boys want to do that, then fine. But count me out."

"That's fine," said Colin. "Whatever you want to do." He shook his head at Wyatt. "Let's finish up here and go home. I've got a shift that starts soon," said Colin.

****

The Tolbert farm was eight miles south of town. The 10-acre land was one of the smallest active farms in the county. In its heyday, it stretched over 80-acres and produced the third-most corn in the county. Cranston Tolbert and his family fell on hard times as droughts and economic downturns forced them to sell off most of their land. Their ramshackle home and dilapidated barn were the only structures still standing.

Wyatt eased his motorcycle up to the entrance of the farm. An aging, wooden gate blocked his view of the house. He rode along the fence until he found a rotted-out opening. He looked through the hole and saw two figures holding rifles in their hands. They were aiming at something in the distance.

Two gunshots pierced the air, followed by two more. The two figures laughed and slapped each other's hands. Wyatt deliberately revved his engine to get their attention. It worked, as the shooters walked toward him with the rifles on their shoulders.

Christopher Tolbert was 22-years-old, with thick arms and a swimmer's build. He led his brother, Karl, who was three years younger, to the opening. Wyatt cut his engine and plastered on a smile. The Tolbert brothers stopped at the opening and suspiciously eyed the intruder. "What the Hell do we have here?" asked Christopher. "A genuine celebrity."

The brothers reeked of beer, and Christopher's words were slightly slurred. Karl snarled at Wyatt and tightened his grip on his weapon. "Good afternoon, fellas," said Wyatt, as he removed his helmet. "Beautiful day, isn't it?" He moved his eyes from brother to brother. "What are you guys up to?" he asked.

"We're shooting our guns, dummy," snapped Karl. His raised his weapon to emphasize his point. "What did you think we were doing?" he asked. He glanced at his brother. "I thought he was supposed to be the smart one."

Christopher shook his head. "No, Colin is the smart boy. He's a police officer." He pointed his rifle at Wyatt. "Wyatt is the numbskull fireman," he said. He took a step toward Wyatt. "I hear you like to start fires. Did you come here to burn our farm down?" he asked.

Wyatt smiled again. "Haven't you heard?" he asked. "I've been exonerated." He raised his hands before dropping them at his sides. "But I'd sure like to find the guy that got me into so much trouble. You wouldn't happen to know anything about that, would you?"

Christopher laughed. "Yeah, we do," he replied. "Karl here is the guilty party. Isn't that right, little brother?" Both brothers laughed. "I was right about to turn him in myself when you showed up. I'm not splitting the reward with you."

Karl spit something nasty onto the grass. "Nah, it wasn't me," he said. "Do me a favor and tell your brother, will you?" he asked. "The sheriff has already questioned me about it."

"I didn't know that," said Wyatt. "Why did he think you did it?" he asked.

"The same reason you think I did," said Karl. He spit again. "Cause I'm a Tolbert, and we aint good for nothing but drinking and stealing and fighting and raising all kinds of Hell." He glanced at Christopher. "Isn't that right, Chris?" he asked.

Christopher frowned. "That's what the townsfolk think," he said. He looked down at his weapon. "And all because we like to have some fun sometimes." He glared at Wyatt. "What do you think, fireman?" he asked.

Wyatt nodded. "I think your family got a raw deal, and the townsfolk find it easy to blame other people before they have all the facts." He paused. "Like they did to me."

Christopher nodded. "Want a beer?" he asked. "We have a full case."

"Another time," said Wyatt. He started his motorcycle's engine. "I have to ride home." He put on his helmet. "Seriously, though. Do you have any idea who might be starting these fires? I want to stop them before someone gets hurt."

"Not a clue," said Christopher. He swatted his brother's shoulder. "We may have done some stuff in the past that isn't quite legal, but burning stuff down isn't one of them. I hope you find this guy. We don't have much, but it's our home and I'd hate to see it go up in flames."

"Take care, guys," said Wyatt. "And be good."

Wyatt sped away from the farm. He turned onto a main highway and cruised toward home. He thought about what Christopher Tolbert said. Wyatt knew the stories about the Tolbert brothers, but never once did they ever do anything involving fire. He was sure they were not the culprits. *Then who the Hell is?* he wondered.

Wyatt was a few miles from town when he saw two cars racing toward him in both lanes. Wyatt jerked his bike to the right and swerved to avoid getting hit. He stopped on the shoulder and turned to see the cars roar by him. They bumped each other and one car screeched out of control. It hit a guardrail on a bridge and plummeted into a lake.

Wyatt pulled out his cell phone. He quickly dialed 911 and told the operator about the accident. He rode up to the broken guard rail and saw the car sinking into the water. Wyatt took off his helmet and dove into the lake.

The shock of the cold water hit him right away. He knew that he didn't have long before his body would give out. He swam to the driver's side door. Inside the vehicle, he saw a kid who couldn't have been more than 16 years old. The driver was unconscious and alone in the vehicle.

Wyatt pulled on the door several times until he pried it open. He reached in and grabbed the driver by the shoulders. He lay the victim over his right shoulder and swam toward the shore. Wyatt felt the numbness spread throughout his body, but he focused on reaching his destination.

He dragged himself and the victim out of the water before he collapsed onto the ground. His entire body shivered as his lungs fought for air. Wyatt turned his head and saw that the driver was still breathing. He blinked his eyes a few times before passing out.

Wyatt woke up on a gurney. An EMT stood over him. Various voices mixed in with the sounds of sirens. It took Wyatt a moment to remember what had happened. He tried to sit up, but the EMT told him to remain still. A different and more familiar voice spoke next. "Wyatt, can you hear me?"

Wyatt focused his eyes and saw Colin standing over him. He slowly nodded. "Get him to the hospital, now!" shouted the deputy. "Wyatt, you are going to be fine."

Wyatt felt himself rolling forward as the gurney moved toward an ambulance. The gurney was carefully raised and put into the vehicle. The doors began to close, but they suddenly stopped. A person hopped into the ambulance and the doors finally closed.

Kasey Carpenter came into Wyatt's sight. Her eyes were wet, and she was shaking. "Wyatt, can you hear me?" she asked. He nodded again. "Oh, thank God," she said. "I heard the call on the radio, and I rushed right over. I'm glad you are alright."

"The driver?" he asked, just above a whisper.

"He's going to make it," said Kasey. "Thanks to you." She laughed and rested her right hand on his. "You know, I still expect you to come to our open house tomorrow," she said. "Don't think this will get you out of it."

"I wouldn't miss it for the world," said Wyatt. He gently squeezed her hand until his eyes closed and everything went dark.

Chapter Eleven

A banner strewn across the front of the Penn Hills Firehouse read *Open House: Free to the Public.* Four red fire trucks were parked on the driveway with red and white balloons tied to them. Firefighters in full gear showed the interested crowd the crucial parts of the vehicles. Wide-eyed children gazed in awe at the axes, the hoses, and the flashing lights on top of the trucks, while the adults chatted with each other in the bright sunshine. Members of the local press attended, with some shooting video footage of the gathering.

Kasey Carpenter greeted the guests as they arrived at the station house. She gave out pamphlets on fire safety, and raffle tickets for an upcoming drawing. The prizes included food baskets, movie tickets, vendor coupons, and firehouse t-shirts. She nervously kept an eye out for Wyatt James as the festivities got underway.

Capt. Sam Carpenter addressed the crowd through a bullhorn. “I want to thank you all for coming out to see us today,” he said. “Your continued support of our brave men and women means a lot to all of us.” He paused and turned to his daughter, who waved at the crowd. “An extra special thanks to Kasey Carpenter for arranging this event.”

The crowd cheered and clapped as Kasey took a step forward. Sam continued his speech. “There will be a raffle later this afternoon. No, you don't need to be here to win,” he added. He walked toward the side of the building. “And as you can see, we have games and food stands set up on the East side for your entertainment. I hope you all have a great time.”

There were more cheers as Sam turned off the bullhorn and handed it to one of the firefighters. The captain mingled with the crowd. He shook hands and stood for pictures with the patrons. His face beamed and it was obvious that he was enjoying the attention.

Kasey drifted through the crowd. She handed out keychains and magnets with the fire station on them. She tried to hide her disappointment when she did not see Wyatt at the event. She bravely held her smile as she answered questions from the visitors.

Nearly an hour into the event, Kasey recognized the sound of a motorcycle approaching the fire house. She pulled away from a droning woman and smiled as she saw Wyatt riding toward her. He parked his motorcycle and turned off the engine. Kasey slowly walked toward him as he took off his helmet.

"Fancy seeing you here today, Mr. James," she said. She reached out and touched the front of his black, leather jacket. She ran her fingers along the smooth material before she glanced down at the bike. "Should you be riding so soon after your heroics?" she asked.

Wyatt smiled and pushed a lock of his hair out of his face. "The doctors cleared me this morning," he said. "I told them I had a date with a pretty firefighter, and that was all they needed." He gently lifted her right hand and kissed the top of it.

Kasey's smile stretched ear-to-ear. She slid her right arm around Wyatt's and guided him toward the festivities. "I am really glad you're here," she said. "I think you will have a great time." They waded through the crowd until they reached a hot dog vender. "How do you like your hot dogs, Wyatt?" she asked. "With mustard or ketchup?"

"Mustard, please," he said. The vendor put a hot dog into a roll, squirted mustard on it, and handed it to Wyatt. "Thank you, sir," he said. Wyatt turned toward Kasey. "How do you like yours?" he asked.

Before Kasey could answer, a woman shoved a microphone into Wyatt's face. Wyatt snapped his head back and put up his right hand. He nearly dropped his hot dog. "What's going on?" he asked. He looked around as a throng of people descended on him. A man in a beat-up tan jacket pointed a television camera at him.

"Wyatt, how do you feel about the arrests to the Tolbert brothers last night?" she asked. "Does it mean that you are completely off the suspect list?" The woman stared straight into Wyatt's eyes with the intensity of a mountain lion chasing its prey.

"What arrests?" he asked. He glanced at Kasey. "What is she talking about?"

A man in a blue topcoat pushed a mobile device at Wyatt. "Are you saying that you didn't know about the arrests?" he asked. Wyatt didn't answer. "When was the last time the police talked to you about the fires?" he asked.

Kasey stepped in front of Wyatt and waved her arms at the crowd. "Wyatt has no comment at this time!" she shouted. She pulled him by his right arm away from the crowd before leading him to the fire house entrance. They rushed into the living room and crashed onto one of the couches.

"That was wild," said Kasey. "I didn't expect them to swarm on you like that."

"Why were the Tolberts arrested?" asked Wyatt. He put his hot dog down on an end table. "They didn't do this," he said. He leaned forward and took a deep breath.

"How do you know that?" asked Kasey. She inched closer to Wyatt. "They have been nothing but trouble their entire lives. I'm surprised they weren't the police's first suspects."

Wyatt shook his head. "I talked to them last night," he said. "Right before the accident. I stopped by their farm because I thought they might have done it too." He glanced around the room before continuing. "I know how most people in town feel about them. And yes, they have been a lot of trouble, but they never burned anything down before. It's not their style."

Footsteps grabbed the attention of Wyatt and Kasey. They both looked up and saw Colin walk into the room. "It might not have been their style, but things change," said Colin. He sat down in a chair near his brother. "I came in here to see if you are alright," he said.

Wyatt nodded. "I'm fine. Tell me what happened last night."

Colin rubbed his neck. "We found them at the old movie theater on 11th Street," he said. "They were throwing rocks at the windows and smashing equipment. We searched their van and found several containers of kerosene. We think the movie theater was the next target." He dropped his hands into his lap.

Wyatt sat back, stunned. "I can't believe it," he said. "I was sure they didn't do it."

Colin cleared his throat. "Wyatt, they confessed last night," he said. "They told us how they planned each fire, and how they stored kerosene on their farm. By the time they were done talking, they were eager to sign their confessions." He leaned over and slapped Wyatt's left shoulder. "Relax, Wyatt," he said. "It's all over. We got the guys, and everyone knows now that you were innocent."

The deputy rose to his feet and picked up Wyatt's hot dog. He took a big bite and slowly chewed it. "Hey, these are really good," he said. "Let's go get some more." He offered Wyatt a hand and helped his brother rise from the couch. He took another bite. "Needs relish, though."

Kasey stood up on her own. "I'm kinda hungry," she said. "I could go for a hot dog." She wrapped an arm around Wyatt's back and guided him out of the living room. "One of the vendors makes funnel cakes. Let's get some of that too."

The trio left the fire house and rejoined the festival crowd. "C'mon, it's this way," said Kasey. She guided the James brothers toward the food vendors. She skipped her feet like a happy child. "I hope they have cinnamon swirl," she said. "That's my favorite."

Kasey came to a dead stop and her expression soured. "Hello, Susan," she said. She tried to smile, but her face froze. "I didn't know you were coming." She glared at Wyatt as he moved up next to her.

"Hi, Wyatt," said Susan Lanford. "How have you been?"

Wyatt looked like a thief caught with jewels in his hands. "Susan. It's good to see you," he said. "You know Kasey Carpenter." Susan nodded. "And my brother, Colin."

Susan shook Colin's hand. The four of them stood in an awkward silence.

"Would you two like a moment alone?" asked Kasey, as she pointed to Wyatt and Susan. They both said no. Kasey nodded. "I'm going to stand in line for my food. I'll be right back." She took a step and then halted. "Colin, would you please come with me?" she asked.

Colin took the hint and walked away with Kasey.

As she stood in line, Kasey kept an eye on Wyatt and Susan. She watched them struggle through their conversation. "I wonder what they are saying," she said to Colin.

"For what it's worth, I don't think they slept together," said Colin. Kasey glared at him. Colin raised his right hand in protest. "I'm just trying to reassure you. My brother isn't someone who hops into bed with just anyone."

"Do you think she is prettier than me?" asked Kasey. She twirled a lock of her hair in her fingers. Kasey's eyes never left the couple. She waited for Colin to reply. "Well, is she?"

Colin laughed. "I'm not stupid," he said. "And I'm not going to answer that question."

"You can tell me the truth," replied Kasey. She lightly punched Colin's right shoulder. "It's not like you and I are an item." They moved up in line. "Tell me."

Colin spoke slowly, as if gathering his thoughts. "If you and Susan were both single, and I were looking for a date, I would choose you," he said. Kasey smiled at Colin. "But do not ever tell my brother I said that."

"Your secret is safe with me," said Kasey. They were nearly at the front of the line, but Kasey's attention remained on Wyatt and Susan. "Why is this taking so long?" she asked. "What could he possibly have to say to her?"

"It looks like he's trying to let her down easy," said Colin. He subtly pointed at Wyatt. "Look how pale his face is," he said. "I hope he doesn't faint."

"If he does, I'll give him some mouth-to-mouth," said Kasey. She ran her tongue along her bottom lip. Kasey watched Wyatt give Susan a quick hug before walking away from her. "Here he comes," she said to Colin. "Act naturally."

The teenage boy behind the food counter asked Kasey what she wanted. Kasey pretended not to see Wyatt as he approached her. "I'd like a cheeseburger, a small fries, and a Coke," she said. The boy nodded and wrote down her order. Kasey finally turned toward Wyatt. "Oh, there you are," she said. "How did it go?"

Wyatt shrugged. "I don't think she'll be calling me anytime soon," he said. He glanced at a copy of the menu that was taped to the counter.

"Glad to hear it," said Kasey, under her breath. "What would you like to eat?" she asked.

Wyatt tapped the menu. "I'd like to get that hot dog," he said. He looked at the teenage boy and give him his full order. Wyatt looked over his shoulder. "Colin, are you still hungry?"

"No, I'm good," said Colin. The lawman peered over at Susan. "Maybe I'll try my luck with Susan," he joked. "Now that she's available."

"That's not funny," said Wyatt. He softly punched his brother's right arm.

Colin punched Wyatt back. "You had your chance," he said. Colin took a step back as Wyatt tried to hit him again. "I'll see you two later," he said, as he walked away.

"Would you really care if he asked Susan out?" asked Kasey. She tried to hide her jealousy, but it was out there for everyone to see.

Wyatt shook his head. "Colin can date whomever he wants," he said. "I just think it would be weird if it were someone that dated me. Even for such a short time."

The counter boy handed Wyatt and Kasey their food. Wyatt paid the bill, and he led the way to an empty table, where they sat down to eat. Neither spoke for a while. They quietly ate their food as Kasey watched patrons pass by them. "It was a good turnout this year," she finally said. "We could sure use the proceeds."

"Yeah, this place is looking a bit haggard," joked Wyatt. He took a sip of his soda. "But with a little paint and some elbow grease, this old barn could really shine." He let out a small laugh. "You're the reason for this year's success. You did a great job planning the event."

"Thank you," said Kasey. She paused and looked into Wyatt's eyes. "The money will help, but what we really need is qualified personnel. Someone with experience who can join us and provide some veteran leadership."

Wyatt sat back and put his cup on the table. He looked away from Kasey. "You sound like you have someone in mind already," he said.

"You know I do," said Kasey. "C'mon, admit it. When you rescued that boy yesterday, there was a part of you that felt a huge rush. Like you could do anything." She reached out and put her left hand over his. "I know that feeling. It comes with the job."

"I didn't think about it," said Wyatt. "When I saw the car sinking, I just reacted. My years of training kicked in." He shook his head. "I don't know that I felt anything in the moment. It was pure instinct."

"That's because you are a natural leader," said Kasey. "It's what makes you a great firefighter, and we need someone like you in our unit."

Wyatt looked down at his feet and grimaced.

"You know that I'm right and that a big part of you misses the job," said Kasey. "Please join us." She gently squeezed his hand. "You won't regret it."

"Maybe you're right," replied Wyatt. He ran his fingers over hers. "Maybe this is what I was meant to do." He let go of her hand and sat back. "What else is there for me? It's too late to join the police force," he joked. He glanced at the people around them before looking back at Kasey. "Give me a little time," he said. "I need that."

"Of course," said Kasey. "You don't have to start right away. Spend some more time with your family, get reacclimated to town. The job will wait for you."

Wyatt rubbed his tired eyes. "There's something else," he said. He leaned toward Kasey. "I don't get why the Tolbert brothers signed confessions. It doesn't make sense."

Kasey grimaced. "You are back on that again?" she asked.

"Hear me out," said Wyatt, as he slowly waved his hands. "The evidence against them was pretty thin. Why would they fold so easily? They have to know that they'd be facing long prison sentences. Why not take their chances in court?"

"Maybe the police interrogators rattled them," said Kasey. She let out small laugh. "C'mon, those two aren't the brightest bulbs in the box. It wouldn't be hard to catch them in a lie." She smiled at Wyatt. "You should be happy about this."

"I'll be happy when I know for certain that we have captured this firebug," he said. He quickly rose to his feet. "I'm sorry, Kasey, but I have to go. There's something I need to do."

Kasey's face sunk. "Where are you going?" she asked.

"I'm going to county lockup," said Wyatt. "I want to talk to the Tolbert brothers. I need to hear their side of the story."

Kasey rose and grabbed Wyatt's jacket. "Wyatt, you are not a police officer," she said. "You don't need to keep investigating this. No one does. The cops have the guys that did it." She paused and let go of his jacket. "It's over, Wyatt."

"I don't think it is," said Wyatt. "And I don't want another fire to start to prove that I'm right. I'm sorry, but I have to go." He turned and started to walk away.

"Then I'm going with you," said Kasey. She sprinted around the table and cut him off.

"No," replied Wyatt. "You need to stay here at the open house." He put his hands on her arms. "This is your big event. You should see it all the through." Wyatt let go of her. "I will give you a call after I come back."

Kasey crossed her arms over her chest. "Wyatt James, if you think I'm going to let you do this without me, you are dead wrong." She sternly stared into his eyes.

Wyatt softened. "Fine," he said. "Have you ever ridden on the back of a motorcycle before?" he asked. He pointed toward his vehicle.

"Sure," said Kasey, with a slight quiver in her voice. "Dozens of times."

"Then, let's go," said Wyatt. He put his right arm around her and guided her toward his motorcycle. He gave Kasey a passenger helmet, and he put on his own.

Kasey sat on the back with her eyes wide open. She tried to keep her hands from shaking, but they started trembling as soon as the Wyatt turned on the engine. She took a deep breath and hugged Wyatt while she said a silent prayer.

Chapter Twelve

The guard behind the front desk chatted on his cell phone as Wyatt and Kasey entered the police station and stopped at the counter. "I don't care what color the bathroom is," said the guard. "I'm only in there for short periods of time." Kasey loudly cleared her throat to get the officer's attention. The lawman raised his index finger at them. "Honey, I don't know why you bother me with these details. You are going to do what you want to no matter what I say."

"Hello, is the sheriff here?" asked Wyatt. He waved his hand at the guard. "This is really important," he said. The guard put a hand over his cell phone. "Hi, thanks," said Wyatt. "Can you tell him that Wyatt James is here?"

"I've got to go, Honey," said the guard. "Work stuff. Bye bye." The guard clicked his cell phone shut. "I'm sorry, Mr. James, but Sheriff Hughes isn't here. He's out on a call."

"That's alright. Maybe you can help me . . ." Wyatt's voice trailed off. He looked at the officers' badge. "Deputy Martin," he said. Wyatt folded his hands and leaned on the counter. "I'd like to see Christopher and Karl Tolbert," he said.

Deputy Martin shook his head. "No sir, I can't help you with that," he said. "Only family members or the suspects' lawyers can speak to them. Sorry."

Kasey stepped forward. "I'm a member of the press," she said. "I'd like to interview them for my publication." She smiled at the officer. "Surely you are aware of the freedom of the press." Her smile widened a bit.

Deputy Martin nodded. "And what publication do you work for?" he asked.

"The Penn Hills Post," she said. "Are you a subscriber?"

The deputy shook his head. "Never heard of them." The lawman opened his cellphone and typed something into the unit. He looked up suspiciously at Kasey. "I don't see anything by that name on the Internet," he stated.

"Well, we are a small, but growing organization," said Kasey. She batted her eyes at the officer. "I'm sure you know that an exclusive interview with the brothers would be a big boost for our circulation." She took a small notebook and a pen out of her purse. "And, of course, we would love a quote from our police department. "It's Deputy Martin, right?" she asked.

The lawman nodded. "Yeah. Dale Martin," he said. He glanced at Wyatt before looking back at Kasey. "C'mon, I'll walk you to their cell." He picked up a set of keys and marched toward the back of the station. Wyatt and Kasey followed him.

"Here they are," said the deputy. They stopped in front of a cell with two occupants. Kasey recognized the Tolbert brothers sitting alone in the cell. "I'll be back in ten minutes," said Deputy Martin.

When the lawman was out of earshot, Wyatt turned to Kasey. "The Penn Hills Post?" he asked. "Really?"

Kasey nodded. "That's the name of our firehouse newsletter," she replied. She gave Wyatt a light shove. "We only have a few minutes," she said. "Talk to them." She put her left hand over her nose to block the smell of urine coming from inside the cell.

Wyatt leaned on the cell door bars. "Hey guys," he said. "I'm Wyatt James and this is Kasey Carpenter. Do you remember me?" he asked.

Christopher approached the duo. "Yeah, you were at our farm the day we got arrested," he said. "You set us up." He tried to grab Wyatt through the bars, but Wyatt quickly stepped back. "I outta break your neck!" shouted Christopher.

"Take it easy, Chris," said Wyatt. He put his hands up in front of him to show Christopher that he was no threat. "I believe you guys, and I'm trying to find out who set you up. It wasn't me."

"How can we believe you?" asked Christopher. "Talking to you got us in here." He banged on the cell door before turning to walk away from the visitors.

Karl slowly approached Wyatt and Kasey. "Chris, I think he's telling the truth," he said to his brother. Karl sized up Wyatt with his eyes. "If he set us up, he wouldn't be here right now. He'd be as far from here as possible." He crossed his arms over his chest. "What do you want to know?" he asked Wyatt.

"Why did you confess to the police?" asked Wyatt.

"Man, we didn't confess," said Karl. "They talked to us in different rooms. We were told that we were going to jail for the rest of our lives unless we signed some pre-written statements," he said. He pressed his lips together. "I don't read too good, and the statements had lots of fancy words in them. I asked if signing them meant we could go home, and the cops said yes."

"Did you ask for a lawyer?" asked Wyatt.

"Hell yeah," replied Karl. "I've seen enough TV shows to ask for a lawyer. The cops kept saying that one was on the way. But they never showed up."

Wyatt looked back at Christopher. “Chris, did they make it clear to you what you were signing?” he asked.

Christopher drifted up next to Karl. “I knew what I was signing,” he said. “But I also knew that if we went to trail, we’d go to jail and never get out. Hell, this town blames us for everything. A jury would convict us in no time.” He paused to spit on the floor. “And yes, I did ask for a lawyer, and they told me the same thing. One was on the way.”

Wyatt nodded. “Look, I’m sorry you guys got caught up in this. I think you’re innocent and I’m going to do whatever I can to prove it,” he said.

Christopher took a step toward Wyatt. “Why do you care what happens to us?” he asked.

Wyatt looked Christopher straight in the eyes. “Because I know what it’s like to be accused of something you didn’t do.” He turned to walk away, but suddenly turned back to face the brothers again. “One last thing. Who led the interrogations?” he asked.

Karl snorted. “Your brother Colin did,” he said. “Didn’t he tell you?” he asked.

“Thank you both for your time,” said Wyatt. He took Kasey by the arm and led her to the front of the police station. Wyatt nodded at Deputy Martin. “We’ll see ourselves out,” he said. They left before Martin could say anything to them.

They walked down the steps toward the street where Wyatt parked his motorcycle. “You really do believe them, don’t you?” asked Kasey. Wyatt nodded. They reached his bike, and he handed her the passenger helmet. He put his on. “What now?” asked Kasey.

“Now we go to the Sheriff Hughes’ office,” said Wyatt. “He’s not out on an assignment, that was just Martin’s way of covering for his boss. He’s been there the entire time.”

"What are you going to tell the sheriff?" asked Kasey.

Wyatt started the motorcycle. "I'm going to tell him that the real arsonist is still out there, and that Penn Hills is not safe. And if he doesn't listen to me, I'll tell the media that the cops have the wrong people in jail. That should put some heat on him to act."

Kasey stood next to the motorcycle with the helmet on. "You know that you don't have to do any of this," she said. "You could let the police handle the case."

"Really?" asked Wyatt. "After all the mistakes they've made, I don't think they will find the real perpetrator." He took a breath. "I'm not even sure they care about the truth. They just want to close the case as quicky as possible."

****

Sheriff Hughes stood outside his office door with his hands on his hips as Wyatt and Kasey entered the county's main police station. The lawman met his visitors at the front desk. "I understand that you have something to tell me, Wyatt," said Hughes.

"Yes, I do, Sheriff," replied Wyatt. "Can we speak in your office?" he asked.

"By all means," said Hughes. He led Wyatt and Kasey inside the office and closed the door behind them. Hughes pointed to two chairs in front of his desk. "Please sit down," he said. Hughes moved to the chair behind his oak desk as his guests got comfortable. "What can I do for you?" he asked.

"I'll get right to it," said Wyatt. He folded his hands in his lap and spoke clearly. "I don't think the Tolbert boys set those fires. I think the real firebug is still out there."

Sheriff Hughes eased back in his chair. "Why do you think that?" he asked.

"I've known the brothers for years," said Wyatt. "And, yes, they are troublemakers, but not arsonists. Think back, Sheriff. They've never been known to burn things. They prefer the thrill of breaking windows and shooting at beer bottles. Arson just doesn't fit."

"And you've come to this conclusion relying on your many years of police work?" asked Hughes. Wyatt started to reply, but Hughes cut him off. "Wyatt, you may be an expert on fighting fires, but when it comes to solving crimes, I'll rely on my officers and their decades of training and experience."

"What about relying on common sense?" said Kasey. The lawman glared at her. "Why would the Tolberts commit these crimes?" she asked. "What do they have to gain? Money? Have you checked their bank records? Do they suddenly have wealth they didn't have before?"

Hughes leaned forward. "I appreciate you coming in to see me about this, but I really don't have time for amateur Hardy boys and Nancy Drews on this case." He pushed a button on his desk and a deputy entered the office. "Please show our guests out," said Hughes.

Wyatt slowly rose to his feet. "Sheriff, I would like to review the tapes of the Tolberts' interrogations," he said. "There seems to be some inconsistencies from what the police say and what the brothers told me today. For instance, they both claim that they asked for a lawyer, yet the questioning continued without either of them getting proper legal counsel."

"Wyatt, you are walking on thin ice here," he said. "Don't make me fine you for interfering in an investigation."

Wyatt pushed on. "Karl said he didn't understand what he was signing when he signed his confession," he added. "I doubt Christopher did as well."

"Those boys had their rights read to them before we asked a single question," said Hughes. He clenched his fists. "And their confessions were obtained legally and properly." He shot to his feet. "I will not have the integrity of my department questioned." Hughes stopped and gathered himself. "The Tolberts are guilty, and they are going to jail. Now go home and stop involving yourself in police business."

The deputy firmly grabbed Wyatt's right arm. "C'mon, boy," he said. "You are no longer welcome here." Wyatt didn't resist, and Kasey followed them toward the office door.

Before she exited, Kasey turned back toward Hughes. "Sheriff, a dangerous arsonist is still on the loose," she said. "You need to catch the real perpetrator before it is too late." Kasey shut the door before she caught up with Wyatt by the front desk. "He doesn't believe us."

"I think he does," said Wyatt. "And I think he is worried that the next fire will kill someone while the Tolberts are locked up." Wyatt peeked back at the closed office door. "If that happens, his career is over. That's what worries him the most."

Wyatt took Kasey by the hand, and they walked out of the police building. They stopped on the steps when Wyatt saw Colin approaching them. He was in full uniform. "What are you two doing here?" he asked.

"We came to talk to the sheriff about the Tolberts," said Wyatt. He let go of Kasey's hand as if expecting a fight to occur. "I don't think they did it, Colin. Things just don't add up."

Colin put up his right hand like a traffic cop. "Technically, I can't discuss an ongoing case with you," he said. "But off the record, the brothers confessed. They did it." He put an arm around Wyatt's right shoulder. "Why can you accept that?" he asked.

"Because it doesn't make any sense," replied Wyatt. He grabbed his brother's police shirt with both hands. "Can't you see? They don't have any motive. They had nothing to gain."

Colin slowly unwrapped Wyatt's fingers from his shirt. "You need to watch your temper, Wyatt," said Colin. "There is only so much I will take from you." He shoved Wyatt away from him. "I'm not just your brother. I am also part of the law in this county."

"You're right, Colin," said Wyatt. He lowered his voice. "I'm sorry. I shouldn't have grabbed you." He took a step toward the lawman. "It's just so frustrating."

"Look, it's out of your hands," said Colin. "A jury will decide if they are guilty and what happens to them." He glanced at Kasey. "You should take this pretty lady out for a bite to eat and let the legal system run its course." He glanced at his watch. "I have to go."

Colin tried to step around Wyatt, but Wyatt cut him off. "Are their confessions legitimate?" asked Wyatt. "Or did you guys violate their civil rights?" He stood toe to toe with Colin, and he didn't budge.

"Are you questioning my honesty?" asked Colin. He shoved Wyatt again. "I am a damn good police officer, and you have no right to treat me this way. I have served this community with honor for years, and no one has ever doubted my work."

"You didn't answer my question, Colin," said Wyatt. "Are those confessions real?"

Colin leaned toward his brother. "If we were alone, I'd kick your ass all over these steps," he said. "Now get out of my way before I arrest you for impeding an investigation." Colin pushed passed Wyatt and stormed up the steps toward the station entrance.

"Are you alright?" asked Kasey. She touched Wyatt's right shoulder. Wyatt shook his head. Kasey wrapped her arm around him. "Give him some time," she said. "He's a good man. He'll do the right thing." She kissed Wyatt's cheek. "After all, he is your brother."

"He may be my brother, but I'm starting to wonder if he is a good man," said Wyatt. He sighed. "If he were involved in any police corruption it would destroy our family. My dad worst of all."

Kasey's cell phone rang. She took a step back and answered it. "Hello? Yes, this is Kasey Carpenter. What?" Her face whitened and her hands suddenly trembled. "When?" She started nodding. "Yes, I'll be right there." She hung up her cell phone and nearly dropped it.

"What's wrong Kasey?" asked Wyatt. "What's happened?" He put his hands on her shoulders to steady her.

Kasey vacantly looked at Wyatt. "It's my father," she said. "He fell at work. An ambulance took him to County General Hospital."

****

Kasey burst through the swinging Emergency Room doors with Wyatt on her heels. She quickly located the admissions desk and she rushed over to it. "My name is Kasey Carpenter," she told the nurse behind the counter. "My father, Sam Carpenter, was brought in not too long ago. Do you know where he is?"

The nurse put her hands on Kasey's. "Honey, I will find out for you," she said. She glanced at Wyatt. "Stay calm and stay with your friend. I will help you." The nurse typed some information into the computer in front of her. She looked up at Kasey. "He is in ER Room 24."

Kasey tore away from the desk. Wyatt had to sprint to catch up to her. She looked at the room numbers until she found the right one. Without looking back, Kasey rushed into Room 24.

She saw her father laying in a hospital bed. An oxygen mask covered his face, and his right leg was elevated with a cast on it. Lance and some of the other firefighters stood around their boss. Kasey moved to the side of the bed. She carefully raised her father's right hand and held it. "Daddy, what happened?" she asked.

Lance inched toward Kasey. "I'm sorry, Kasey," he said. "It's all my fault. Your dad was on a ladder when he had a heart attack." Lance's eyes welled up. "I never should have let him get on the ladder, but he insisted on cleaning the glass on the station's front door."

Kasey's head snapped up at Lance. "He had a heart attack?" she asked.

Lance barely spoke. "Yes, I'm afraid so." He started crying again. Kasey reached out and hugged him. "I'm so sorry, Kasey," said Lance. "I wish there was something I could do."

A doctor in a white coat entered the sparse room. "Are you Mrs. Carpenter?" he asked Kasey. She nodded as she pulled away from Lance. "I'm Dr. Fullerton," said the physician. He opened a folder in his hands. "I'm afraid your father has blockages in 3 of his arteries. He is stable now, but his going to need surgery."

The doctor took a piece of paper out of the folder and handed it to Kasey. "We are going to need your consent before we can operate."

Kasey wiped her eyes as she tried to read the consent form. She was so upset that she couldn't focus on the words on the page. She rushed through the reading and asked if the doctor had a pen. He handed her one, and Kasey quickly signed the form.

The doctor lowered his voice as if trying to calm Kasey. "We have an operating room ready for him," he said. "We will be taking him down in just a few minutes." He paused and touched Kasey's right shoulder. "I know how frightening this can be, but we have the finest doctors in the state at this hospital. We will do everything we can for your father."

"Thank you, doctor," said Kasey. The physician turned and left the room.

Lance addressed the other firefighters. "Let's go, guys," he said. "Kasey needs her privacy." He ushered out his coworkers and he turned to face Kasey again. "Kasey, if you need anything at all, call me," he said.

Kasey nodded at Lance before she returned to her father's side. She held his hand again as her body shook.

Wyatt eased over to her. "Your father is a strong man," he said. "He'll get through this." Wyatt wrapped his right arm around Kasey. "Before you know it, he'll be back at the firehouse leading the unit." He gently kissed the top of her head.

"I hope so," said Kasey. She wept more. "I don't know what I would do without him. He is the greatest man I've even known." She rubbed her eyes. "I wish I had told him that."

Wyatt hugged her. "You can tell him that when he comes home."

They stood silently watching the fire chief. His chest rose and fell with each breath. Behind him, a machine beeped as lines ran across a screen. The room was chilly, and a thin blanket was all that covered the unconscious man.

A young doctor and two orderlies entered the room. “I’m Dr. Grant,” said the physician. “We are here to take Mr. Carpenter to surgery.” He stopped next to Kasey and glanced at her face. “If you need a moment more, we can wait for you,” he said.

“No,” said Kasey. “I don’t want to get in the way.” She moved toward Wyatt and watched the medical crew slowly wheel her father out into the hall. Kasey and Wyatt followed the gurney down the hall to the elevators. There wasn’t enough room for all of them to fit, so Kasey gently squeezed Wyatt’s hand as she watched the elevator doors close.

Kasey fell into Wyatt’s arms again. She cried as her mind was flooded with images of her father. Wyatt remained quiet and held her closely. Other people passed them, but neither moved from their spots. They seemed rooted to the floor.

Finally, Kasey let go of Wyatt and stepped back. “I’m going to the visitors lounge,” she said. She wiped her eyes again. “You don’t have to stay if you don’t want to. It’s going to be a very long night.”

“If you don’t mind, I’d like to stay,” said Wyatt. “I’m here for you for however long you need me.” They hugged again. Wyatt led Kasey to the visitors lounge and they sat down next to each other. The room was nearly empty, and the sound of the television boomed off the walls.

Wyatt sat with Kasey for several hours as they waited for news about her father. Exhaustion got the best of Wyatt, and he fell asleep first. Kasey watched him sleep and she wondered how she could be so lucky and so unlucky at the same time.

Chapter Thirteen

The dust swirled around Wyatt's face as he swept dirt out of the garage and onto the grass beside the driveway. The simple chore was a therapeutic way of putting aside his problems for a little while. The solitude was a bonus. He needed some peace and quiet. He needed to keep the noise of life at bay for as long as he could.

Wyatt finished cleaning the floor and he put the broom back on the hook in the rear of the garage. He stopped and looked at several items that hung on that part of the wall. There were gloves, shovels, tools, a hedge trimmer, a gas-powered blower, and an old ten-speed bicycle on hooks on the wall. Everything had a place, and everything was in its place. David James was an organized man, and his garage was proof of that.

Two rows of boxes were neatly stacked along the back of the garage, leaving just enough room for David to park his car inside it. Wyatt bent down and opened a box. Inside were dishes and utensils wrapped in newspapers. He opened another box and found some old toys that he and Colin had played with during their childhood. Wyatt took out some action figures and he marveled at how well preserved they were.

The solitude ended as the door to the laundry room opened. David James stepped into the garage and stopped suddenly. "I didn't know you were out here," he said. He shut the door behind him. "What are you doing with those boxes?" he asked.

Wyatt put the action figures back inside the box. "Just reminiscing, I guess," he replied. He closed the box and opened another. Inside were more toys. "I'm surprised you kept this stuff all these years," he said. "I know how much you hate clutter."

"Your mother never thought of this stuff as clutter," said David. He pulled open a lawn chair and sat down in it. "I guess she couldn't bring herself to throw anything out that belonged to you boys," he said. "She was sentimental that way."

Wyatt smiled at the thought of his mother. "Yeah, she loved to keep stuff. That's why the attic is full, and these boxes are down here." He sifted through the open box. "Mom never wanted us to toss anything that we might want in the future."

"What I don't understand is how anyone got into this garage and planted those kerosene containers without my noticing," said David. "I'm still pretty sharp for a man my age. I don't know how I didn't see them."

Wyatt shrugged. "If someone wants to do something bad enough, they usually find a way," he said. "Anyone could overlook something as innocuous as small metal containers. They don't really jump out at you."

"For what it's worth, Wyatt," said David. "I never believed that you set those fires. You are a damn good human being, and you would never deliberately destroy anything. Hell, you are a firefighter, not a firebug."

Wyatt looked over at his father. "Thanks, Dad," he replied. "I'm glad that you feel that way." He wanted to hug the man, but he knew that would make his father uncomfortable, so he stayed put. Wyatt pushed the toys around inside the box until he found a small, red firetruck. He lifted it up and showed it to David. "Hey Dad, remember this?" he asked.

David smiled. "Your mother gave you that when you were eight-years-old," he said. He shook his head. "Boy, you carried that around with you all the time. You even held onto it when you slept in bed." David paused and pressed his lips together. "When you decided to become a firefighter, your mother was extremely proud of you. So was I."

"What about Colin?" asked Wyatt. "Are you proud of him too?"

"Of course, I am," said David. "I'll admit, I was a little disappointed that he chose law enforcement over firefighting, but his is a noble job too." David laughed. "It's funny, he had a fascination with fire as a kid. I guess it just never stayed with him."

Wyatt put the toy back into the box. "I always admired you, Dad," said Wyatt. "You were a firefighter, the best in town. I wanted to be just like you. How could I not follow in your footsteps?" He paused and remembered his father in his firefighting gear. "I've been doing this my whole life. I can't imagine doing anything else."

"Does that mean you are going to join the Penn Hills fire company?" asked David. He folded his fingers together and rested his hands in his lap. "I know that pretty Kasey Carpenter has been after you to work for them. I think it's a great opportunity."

Wyatt sighed. "I haven't decided yet," he said. He rubbed his eyes. "I don't even know if I can do it anymore, Dad," he said. Wyatt pulled up a stool and sat down on it. "What good is a firefighter who is afraid?" he asked.

David leaned toward his son. "What are you afraid of?" he asked. "You've put out hundreds of fires already. You know how to take care of yourself."

"But do I know how to take care of my coworkers?" he asked.

David shook his head in frustration. "As usual, Wyatt, I don't know what the Hell you're talking about." He tapped Wyatt's right shoulder with the back of his hand. "Care to enlighten me?" he asked.

Wyatt looked at his father and fought back tears. He told David about the fire that killed Duane Wright in Ohio. "I still have nightmares about it, Dad," he said. "It was my fault. If I had stayed with him, he'd be alive today."

"You don't know that for certain," said David. He rested a hand on his son's shoulder. "If you had stayed with him, all three of you might have died. You decided that the child's safety was the most important thing. That was the right decision." He pulled his hand back. "I would have done the same thing."

David wiped his eyes again. "Even if you are right, how do I live with it?" he asked. "How do I ask another firefighter to trust me with their life again?"

"There is no easy answer, Wyatt," said David. "All you can do is get up every day, breathe, go to work, and do your best to help people. You learn from your mistakes and try not to repeat them." He cleared his throat. "But understand, you will lose other firefighters in the future. That's part of the business."

Wyatt looked at his father. "How many firefighters did you lose," he asked.

David shook his head. "Too many." He looked down at the floor. "I can see their faces in my mind. But we honor those we've lost by continuing to do our job to the best of our abilities." He nodded enthusiastically. "Think about all the people we've saved over the years. That's why we do the job."

"I guess so," said Wyatt. "Dad, I'm sorry I wasn't around more, especially after Mom got sick," he said. "I should have been here for her. And for you and Colin." He offered his father his right hand. David reached out and shook it.

"I can't really blame you," said David. "There were plenty of times when I was away from your mother for too long." He slowly stood and put his chair back. "I know what this job does to a person. It takes so much time and energy."

Wyatt returned his chair and followed David inside the house. "There's a hockey game on TV," said David. "Want to watch it with me?" he asked. David stopped at the refrigerator and took out two bottles of beer. He turned and handed one to Wyatt.

"Sure, that sounds like fun," said Wyatt. "Thanks." He opened the bottle took a sip. "How are the Flyers looking this year, Dad?" he asked.

David led the way to the living room. "Not so great, really," he said. "Same old thing each year: We have a solid goaltender but no one to score for us." David sat on the couch and Wyatt dropped into a comfortable chair. David turned on the television. "Oh, good, they're just getting started."

Father and son watched the first period together. David gave his commentary on the game, while Wyatt kept mostly quiet and enjoyed the time with his dad. Wyatt thought back to the games they used to watch together when he was a kid. Win or lose, Wyatt always had fun watching David cheer on the home team.

Colin came home and entered the living room during the second period. "Hey Dad," he said. He sat on the couch next to David, but he ignored Wyatt. "How bad are we losing?"

"The Rangers are up by two goals," replied Wyatt. Colin glanced at him without speaking. Wyatt stood up and offered his hand to Colin. "Hi, I'm Wyatt James," he said. "I used to be a firefighter, but the last fire I fought really shook my confidence." He paused. "And I'm also your older brother."

Colin slapped away Wyatt's hand. "Sit down, dumbass, I know who you are," said Colin. "But before you go, grab me a beer." Colin leaned back in his seat. "A cold one."

Wyatt returned to his seat. "I'm not your butler, junior," said Wyatt. "Get your own damn beer." He crossed his arms over his chest. "Just make sure you read it its rights before you drink it. And don't rough it up."

Colin shot to his feet. "That's enough, tough guy!" he snapped. "I'm not taking your crap at work and I'm not taking it here." He took a step toward Wyatt, who rose with his fists clenched. "Maybe we should step outside!" yelled Colin.

"Anytime, short stuff," said Wyatt.

David stood up and grabbed Colin's left arm. "Knock it off, both of you!" he shouted. He pulled Colin toward him and shoved him back down on the couch. David glared at Wyatt. "Sit down!" he ordered. Wyatt did so. "I don't know what's going on with you boys, but you need to settle it like gentlemen. Like brothers. Not Neanderthals."

Neither son spoke. They both knew better than to openly challenge their father.

"Whatever the problem is, I want you to apologize to each other," said David. "Shake hands and put an end to it." Neither James boy moved. "Right now!" yelled David.

Wyatt slowly rose to his feet and offer his hand again. Colin remained seated but shook Wyatt's hand. They glared at each other for a moment before releasing from the handshake. Wyatt sat down and looked at the television. During their screaming match, the Flyers let in another goal. Wyatt shook his head.

"That's better," said David. He ambled away from his sons and spoke over his right shoulder. "I got hit the can," he said. "When I come back, I better not find any blood on the floor, if you know what's good for you."

Wyatt waited until David was out of the room. He rose and quietly walked out of the living room, and out the front door. Wyatt took out his cell phone and called Kasey. "Hey, it's Wyatt," he said to her. "Can I see you now? I really need to."

****

Sam was sitting up in bed and sipping water through a straw when Wyatt entered the hospital room with a stuffed bear in his hands. Kasey sat in a chair next to the bed. She leaped up and rushed over to Wyatt. She wrapped her arms around him. "Thank you for coming," she said. She kissed his cheek. "I'm really glad you're here."

Wyatt kissed her back and eased away from her. He watched Sam put the cup of water down on a nearby table. "You're looking better, Chief," he said. He handed Sam the bear. "I didn't think you'd want flowers," he said.

Sam smiled as he looked at the bear. It was brown and dressed up as a firefighter. "Thank you, Wyatt," he said. The men shook hands. "Call me Sam. By the looks of it, you are nearly family now."

Kasey blushed. “Dad,” she said. She pulled another chair over toward hers, and she and Wyatt sat down. “We were just talking about the case,” she said to Wyatt. “Dad agrees with you. The arrest of the Tolberts doesn’t make sense.”

Wyatt nodded. “So, who does that leave?” he asked Sam.

The fire chief shook his head. “I don’t know. But the usual motives for arson are money, murder, or revenge.” He scratched his chin. “Who is benefitting from these fires?”

“That’s what I’ve been wondering,” said Wyatt. He rubbed his hands together. “You shouldn’t be worrying about this now,” he said to Sam. “You just focus on getting better. The real firebug will be caught. It’s just a matter of time.”

Sam yawned and laid his head back onto his pillow. “I guess you’re right, Wyatt,” he said. Sam closed his eyes. “If you two don’t mind, I am feeling kinda tired.”

“No problem, Dad,” said Kasey. She rose and kissed Sam on the forehead. “I’ll stop by later to check on you.” She adjusted his blanket for him. “Love you, Dad,” she said.

“Love you, too,” said Sam. He turned his head on his pillow before falling asleep.

Kasey took Wyatt by the arm and led him out of the hospital room. Once they were in the hallway, she hugged Wyatt again. “He’s going to be okay, isn’t he?” she asked.

“Yes,” said Wyatt. “Your father is a strong man. He’ll bounce back in no time.” He felt her body shake as she began to sob. “It’s alright, Kasey,” he said. Wyatt hugged her tightly. “Sam is going to be fine.”

Kasey pulled away and wiped her eyes. "I know. It just scares me to see him like this," she said. "Even for a little while." She patted Wyatt's right shoulder. "C'mon, I'll buy you lunch," she said. "I need to get back to the station anyway."

Wyatt followed Kasey to the fire station. He parked his motorcycle and followed her inside the building. Her coworkers sat in the living room watching television. Lance rose to greet them. "Hey Kasey," he said. Lance offered a hand to Wyatt. "Wyatt, it's good to see you again."

"Thank you," said Wyatt. They shook hands. "It's good to be here."

"Kasey, how is your father doing?" asked Lance.

"He's hanging in there," she said. She lightly touched Lance's right shoulder. "Thanks for asking." She waved Lance and Wyatt over to a quiet corner of the room. "With my dad in the hospital," she said to Lance. "You are now the acting fire chief."

Lance nodded. "Yeah, I know." He pressed his lips together. "And I hope Sam gets back here soon," he said. "I don't know how the others will react when the time comes."

Wyatt looked at Lance. "Just be firm and confident," he said. "Show them that and they will follow you."

"Thanks, Wyatt," said Lance. He pointed toward the television. "I'm going get back to the movie. Goose just died and Maverick isn't handling it well." He walked away and sat down on the couch with his buddies.

Kasey and Wyatt walked into the kitchen. "I'm going to make myself a ham and cheese sandwich," said Kasey. "Want one?" She moved toward the refrigerator to take out the food.

"Yeah, that sounds good," said Wyatt. He leaned against a counter and watched Kasey put their lunch together. "Lance seems nice," he said. "Are you two friends?" he asked.

Kasey nodded. "You know how it is in a firehouse," she said. "We all get pretty close." She took a knife out of a drawer. "Do you want mustard or mayo?" she asked.

"Mustard is fine," said Wyatt. "He looked really happy to see you. Is there anything going on there?" he asked. He walked to the refrigerator and took out a can of soda.

Kasey smiled at him. "Hey, are you jealous?" she asked. Wyatt shrugged. Kasey moved to him and wrapped her arms around his neck. "That is sweet," she said. She kissed him and hugged him tightly. "No, there is nothing going on there," she said.

"Good," said Wyatt. He kissed her and touched her shoulders. "I really care about you, Kasey," he said. "I can see us being something special together." They embraced again until someone entered the kitchen and cleared their throat.

Wyatt pulled back and saw Lance standing by the coffee machine. "Sorry to interrupt," he said. "But I did want to talk with both of you."

Kasey smiled at Lance. "Sure," she said. "What's on your mind?"

"I don't want to overstep my bounds," said Lance. "But with Sam out, we are even more understaffed." He looked at Wyatt. "Wyatt, I know that you were a firefighter in Ohio. Would you like to join our staff? We could really use someone like you."

Wyatt glanced at Kasey. She shook her head. "No, I didn't put him up to this," she said. "But Lance is right. We need you. What do you say?"

Wyatt leaned against a counter. "Do you know why I came back to town?" he asked.

Kasey nodded. "For your mother's funeral," she said.

"Not just that," said Wyatt. He took a deep breath and told them about the fire that killed Duane Wright. Kasey's eyes filled with tears as he finished. "I know you had a similar thing happen to you, Kasey," said Wyatt. "But my partner died and I'm having a lot of trouble dealing with it. I don't know if I can rush into a burning building again."

"Man, I'm sorry," said Lance. "I had no idea. I wouldn't have asked you."

Wyatt shook his head. "It's not your fault," he said. "I appreciate the offer. Lord knows I need a job. I just don't know how good I would be."

"I understand," said Lance. "But the offer still stands. Whatever you want to do is fine with me." He shook Wyatt's hand again before leaving the kitchen.

Wyatt and Kasey at their lunch in the kitchen. Neither said much. Wyatt cleaned up after they finished. Kasey walked up behind him and hugged him. "Whatever you decide is fine with me too," she said. "I want what's best for you."

The fire alarm went off. Kasey and the others scrambled to get dressed and get the fire trucks moving. Wyatt calmly walked over to Lance as he got ready. "You got room for one more?" he asked. Lance smiled and gathered a suit and gear for Wyatt.

Wyatt dressed quickly and joined Kasey on one of the firetrucks. The vehicle roared onto the road with its siren blasting. Kasey lightly punched Wyatt's shoulder and nodded at him. He nodded back. Wyatt took a deep breath and prayed for the strength to do his best.

Chapter Fourteen

The firetruck screeched to a halt in front of the apartment complex. The firefighters hopped out of the truck and gathered around Lance. “Listen up!” he shouted. “We have flames on the first and second floors. Delta team set up the hoses, Omega team let’s get inside and clear the building.” He clapped his hands. “Let’s go!” he yelled.

Wyatt was on the Omega team, so he followed Kasey and Lance toward the entrance of the building. Before they ran in, Lance turned to Wyatt. “Are you sure you’re up to this?” he asked. Wyatt took a deep breath and nodded. “Okay, here we go,” said Lance. He led his team inside the expanding inferno.

The heat hit Wyatt like a tidal wave. His eyes burned from the smoke that enveloped the hallway. The firefighters used their flashlights to find their way. They yelled out for anyone trapped in the building. Muffled screams came from all directions. Lance and a firefighter named Colby went in one direction, two others went in another, while Wyatt closely followed Kasey.

Wyatt’s heart pounded in his chest. He focused on slowing his breathing. He and Kasey called out to anyone in need. They followed the sounds of a person hollering for help. Wyatt pushed through broken furniture and fallen debris until he found a man trapped under a beam. “Over here!” he yelled to Kasey.

The firefighters lifted the beam off the man, and they pulled him toward an open space in the room. There was a large gash on the man’s forehead. “We’ve got to get him out of here,” said Kasey. They put the man’s arms over their shoulders, and they carefully guided him out of the building. An EMT met them on the sidewalk, and the man was placed onto a gurney.

Wyatt and Kasey took off their masks to breathe fresh air. They stood facing each other for a minute before Kasey put her mask back on. Wyatt did the same and followed her back into the burning building. He told himself not to let her get more than two strides away from him.

Their search and rescue continued. The fire crackled around them like thunder. They ventilated the building as best they could while calling out for survivors. Wyatt's right foot bumped against something. He stopped and pointed his flashlight downward. He cringed when he saw the charred body.

Kasey moved toward him. She pointed her flashlight at the body. She bent down and examined it more closely. Kasey slowly stood back up. "She's dead," said Kasey. "We'll come back for her if we can. C'mon, we have a lot of ground to cover."

They resumed their pursuit of survivors. Wyatt's legs ached and he was surprised at how out of shape he had become so quickly. He ignored the pain in his legs and back as he and Kasey cleared room after room. Wyatt realized that their oxygen tanks were getting low, so he tried to pick up the pace.

Wyatt exited a room when the floor above him collapsed. He dove to avoid the falling debris. Wyatt landed with a thud on the floor. He scrambled to his feet and called out to Kasey. She called back that she was okay. Wyatt froze as thoughts of Duane Wright filled his mind. He forced himself to keep moving forward.

They met up with Lance and Colby. "We've finished our section," said Lance. "How are you two doing?" he asked. He directed his question at Kasey, but Wyatt knew Lance was really asking about him. Kasey gave him a thumbs up. "Good," said Lance. "We need to clear out and refill our air tanks," he said.

The team moved in a two-by-two formation as they slogged through the burning structure. Wyatt knew that any footstep could lead to disaster, so he pressed his feet carefully on the unstable floor. The firefighters were near the front door when Wyatt heard a rhythmic thumping below him. He immediately stopped and alerted the others.

"Did you check the basement?" he asked Lance.

The leader shook his head. "No, not yet," he said.

The thumping grew louder. "I think there's someone down there," said Wyatt. He turned and saw a door leading to the basement. "I'm going to take a look."

"I'll go with you," said Kasey. "For backup."

Lance moved toward them. "We'll all go," he said. "But remember that we don't have much time. This place is going to fall in on itself."

"I saw a door over there," said Wyatt. He rushed over to the door, but slowly opened it. He turned back to the group. "Yeah, it goes downward." He adjusted his mask and rushed down the steps. The team followed him.

Wyatt focused his hearing on the sound he heard earlier. The basement was dark and filled with junk, which made it difficult to navigate. He soon heard the thumping again. "It's coming from over there," he said, pointing toward the near wall.

Wyatt tripped over a set of skis, but he kept his balance and reached a small door. He turned the knob, but it was locked. "Hello!" he shouted. "Is a anyone in there?" He pounded on the door. "We're firefighters. We're here to help!"

There was no response. Wyatt took an axe from one of his coworkers and he cut open the door. He peeked inside and saw a little girl. She wore pink pajamas and rocked back and forth in fear. “It’s okay,” said Wyatt. “We won’t hurt you. Take my hand.”

The girl extended her arms. Wyatt had to stretch as far as he could to reach her. Their fingers touched and he gently pulled her out of the tiny closet. Wyatt handed the girl to Kasey.

“Let’s get out of here,” said Lance. He led the squad toward the steps. Wyatt was last in line. He saw something move in a far corner.

“You go,” he said to the crew. “I think there’s someone over there.” Wyatt pushed aside burning boxes and trudged to the other side of the room. He looked down and saw a man buried under fallen debris. He dug the man out and froze when he recognized the man’s face. It was Colin.

Wyatt snapped back to reality, and he lifted his brother off the floor. He carried him toward the exit. He was nearly back in line with the others when he saw a hand sticking out from under a pile of rags. “We’ve got another one over there!” he yelled.

Lance rushed past Wyatt and stopped over the fallen figure. Lance scooped up a man wearing fire-retardant clothing and he followed the others up the steps. The tricky maneuvering took extra time. Wyatt started feeling lightheaded. He realized that he was nearly out of oxygen, and that the others must be too.

Wyatt heard the creaking sound of metal collapsing. Pieces of the ceiling rained down on the firefighters as they struggled to reach the front door. A chunk of wood hit Wyatt in the back of his right leg, but he ignored the pain and pushed through to the exit.

Once outside, the firefighters placed the victims on gurneys. EMTs examined the survivors. Wyatt stayed close to his brother, while Lance kept an eye on the man he rescued. Colin was given oxygen as Wyatt watched an EMT checked out the lawman.

"How bad is he?" asked Wyatt. He realized he was crowding the EMT, so he took a step back. "Is he going to live?" he asked.

The EMT nodded at Wyatt. "His injuries don't appear to be serious," said the first responder. "But we need to get him to the hospital."

Colin slipped off his mask. "The guy in the fire suit," he said. "Is he still alive?"

Wyatt looked over at the man Lance rescued. A different EMT was working on him. "Yeah, he doesn't look too bad," said Wyatt. He turned to face Colin. "What the Hell were you two doing in the building?" he asked.

"That's our firebug," said Colin. He sat up and looked in the man's direction. Colin coughed. "I got a tip from a snitch that this place was the next target," he said. "When I got here, I found the place on fire, and I went in to find the arsonist."

"What?" asked Wyatt. "You rushed into a burning building by yourself with no equipment?" Colin shrugged. "Are you nuts? You could have been killed."

"That's not the strangest part," said Colin. "When I found the guy, he was unconscious on the floor. Did you see the gash on the back of his head? He was hit from behind while he was still inside," said Colin. "Someone else was with him and tried to kill him." Colin coughed again.

"That's enough," said the EMT. "He has to go to the hospital."

Wyatt nodded and put the mask back over Colin's face. "Don't worry, if he is awake, I'll talk to him," said Wyatt. He helped load the gurney into an ambulance. The vehicle took off with its lights flashing and its siren screaming.

Wyatt walked over to the arsonist's gurney. The man's eyes were open, and he was trying to talk. Lance leaned over and tried to catch what the man was saying. Lance straightened up when he saw Wyatt standing next to him. "How is your brother?" asked Lance.

"The EMT said he'll be fine, but he still had to go to the hospital," said Wyatt. "Colin said that this guy is our firebug." He filled Lance in on the other details. "Does he have a gash on the back of his head?" asked Wyatt.

Lance helped the man sit up. He and Wyatt both saw the wound. "What happened to you?" asked Lance.

"I aint talking till I see my lawyer," said the suspect.

"Do you always hang out in burning buildings with a fire suit?" asked Wyatt. He touched the material on the man's right sleeve. "This doesn't look like dinner attire," he added.

"I got nothing to say," said the man. He laid down on the gurney and closed his eyes.

"We need to get him to the hospital," said the man's EMT.

Lance nodded and told them to go. He turned to face Wyatt as Kasey joined them. "We have a job to finish," said Lance. "We're going to help Delta team put out these flames." The leader marched toward the truck with Wyatt and Kasey behind him.

The team spent the next hour extinguishing the flames and putting out hotspots. When they finished, Wyatt saw Sheriff Hughes speaking with Lance. The lawman looked worried.

Wyatt walked over to the sheriff. "Sheriff Hughes, what do we know about the suspect?" he asked. "And how soon will the Tolbert brothers be released?"

"Hold on, Wyatt," said Hughes. He nervously looked around at the fire scene. "We don't have all the facts yet. It could be that this guy you found was working with the Tolberts the entire time." He started to walk away, and Wyatt followed him. "We're not releasing anyone yet."

"What happened when you questioned the suspect?" asked Wyatt.

Hughes stopped walking and turned to face Wyatt. "He lawyered up," he said. He rubbed his neck. "I left the hospital when his attorney arrived. But he's not going anywhere. He is handcuffed to his bed, and I posted a guard outside his door."

Another deputy approached the sheriff and whispered into his ear. Hughes looked at his underling. "Are you sure?" asked Hughes. The deputy nodded. "Fine, let's go." The sheriff and his deputy raced toward the police cars. They go into their respective vehicles and took off.

****

Wyatt and Kasey went to the hospital after their shift ended. They said hello to Sam first before going to see Colin. The deputy was in a single room. He held a remote control in his hand, and he flipped through the television channels. He put the device down when he saw his visitors. "Hey, I thought you forgot about me," he joked.

"Never," said Wyatt. He approached the side of the bed and gently shook hands with his brother. "You don't look so bad," he said. "Just a little char broiled."

Colin laughed. "Yeah, now I know what a slice of bacon feels like," he said.

“What did the doctors say about you?” asked Kasey. She carefully sat on the bed. Wyatt grabbed a chair and slid it close to his brother. He sat down as Colin laid back on a pillow.

“I had some smoke inhalation, and a few cuts and bruises,” said Colin. “But I’ll live.” He blinked a few times. “I really want to question that firebug,” he said. “I’m sure I could get him to crack.” He punched his left hand with his right fist. The cracking sound startled Wyatt.

“I’m afraid that wouldn’t help,” said Wyatt. “He asked for a lawyer.”

“The guilty ones always do,” said Colin. “He was working for someone, I’m sure of that. We just need to find out who that someone is,” he said. He took a deep breath. “You know, I am getting a bit dizzy,” he said. “Maybe I should get some rest.”

“That’s a great idea, Colin,” said Wyatt. He rose from his chair and helped Kasey to her feet. Wyatt pushed the chair back against the wall. “You get some sleep, and we’ll stop by tomorrow to visit you.”

Colin nodded and he was soon fast asleep. Wyatt took Kasey by the hand and guided her out to the hallway. “Colin’s right,” said Wyatt. “We need to find out who hired the firebug before he finds someone else to finish the job.”

“How do we do that?” she asked. “We can’t go right up to him and ask.”

Wyatt smiled. “Why not?” he asked. “We are not members of law enforcement. Where does it say that we can’t talk to him?” asked Wyatt. “Let’s see if he is awake.” He moved toward the arsonist’s room with Kasey right behind him.

The state trooper guarding the arsonist's room rose from his chair as Wyatt and Kasey approached. "Can I help you?" he asked, in a deep voice. The trooper stood a few inches taller than Wyatt, and he was built like a professional football player.

Wyatt and Kasey removed their ID's and showed them to the officer. The trooper shook his head. "This is a restricted area," he said. "I'm going to have to ask you to leave." He took a step toward them, but Wyatt and Kasey stood their ground. The trooper stopped. "Do we have a problem here?" he asked. He put his right hand on his weapon.

"No, no problem," said Kasey. She slowly put her ID away. "Look, this is Wyatt James. His brother is Deputy Colin James." She pointed behind her. "Colin is in Room 12. He is the one who caught this guy. We just want to ask him a few questions."

"I have my orders, Ma'am," said the trooper. He removed his hand from his pistol. "Please leave." He pointed in the direction they came from. Neither firefighter moved. "Don't make me arrest you," said the trooper.

"No one is getting arrested," said a voice. Wyatt and Kasey turned to see Sheriff Hughes walking toward them. "Trooper, I can vouch for these two." He turned toward the firefighters. "Hello Wyatt," he said. He shook hands with Wyatt and Kasey. "Kasey, always nice to see you." Hughes pointed toward the hospital door. "Trooper, open that door."

The state trooper did as he was told. Wyatt and Kasey followed Sheriff Hughes into the room. The suspect was awake in bed, eating a red apple. "What are you doing here?" he asked. "I'm waiting for my lawyer to come back. Till then, I aint saying anything."

"Relax, Fassel," said Hughes. "This isn't a formal meeting. I'm just here to make sure you haven't accidentally hurt yourself or anything. It would be a real shame if you didn't get your day in court."

"Fassel?" asked Wyatt. "Is that your name?"

The sheriff nodded. "Wyatt James, meet Brendon Fassel. Arsonist, thief, mugger, and all-around scumbag." Hughes laughed. "Fassel here has a rap sheet as long as your arm. He is the reason this town turned against you not too long ago."

"Stop," said Fassel. "You're hurting my feelings." He took a bite of his apple.

"Why did you do it, Fassel?" asked Wyatt. "Why did you set those fires?"

"No lawyer, no comment," said Fassel. He finished his apple and tossed it into a trashcan. Fassel pointed toward the door. "Now get the Hell out!" he shouted.

Sheriff Hughes moved closer to Fassel, and the suspect flinched. Wyatt and Kasey both noticed. "Watch your mouth, boy, or I'll smack it shut!" snapped Hughes. The lawman quickly regained his composure. "Figuratively speaking."

Wyatt inched closer to Fassel. "You don't look smart enough to pull this off on your own," he said. "Who were you working for? Who paid you to do this?" asked Wyatt. He rushed the suspect and grabbed him by the shoulders. "Who paid you?" he screamed.

Hughes and Kasey both grabbed Wyatt and pulled him off Fassel. "What the Hell are you doing, Wyatt?" asked Hughes. Wyatt fell to the floor and remained there for a moment. He slowly got up and glared at Fassel. "Get him out of here," said Hughes.

Kasey took Wyatt by the arm and led him out of the room. “What’s wrong with you?” asked Kasey. “You can’t go off on someone like that. It could cost you your career.”

Wyatt smiled and guided Kasey away from the state trooper. “I think I know who Fassel is working for,” he said. They sat down in two chairs along a far wall. “You saw the way Fassel reacted when Hughes got close to him?” he asked.

Kasey nodded. “Yeah, he nearly jumped out of his skin.”

“Exactly,” said Wyatt. “I think Hughes hired Fassel to set those fires. And Fassel is terrified of the sheriff, because Hughes tried to kill him in the last fire.”

“Why would the sheriff want to set the fires?” asked Kasey. “It doesn’t make sense.”

“It does if he did it to try to collect insurance money,” said Wyatt. “The last fire was at a delipidated apartment complex. Maybe he owns it.”

Kasey shook her head. “That’s pretty thin, Wyatt,” she said. “I know you don’t like the guy, but that doesn’t make him an arsonist. Or a killer.” She put a hand on his right shoulder. “He’s a lawman. Like your brother.”

“Maybe so, but it makes sense,” said Wyatt.

A voice came over the loudspeaker. “Code Blue in Room 17. Code Blue in Room 17.”

A group of doctors and nurses dashed down the hallway toward the state trooper. He stood and let them enter the room. Wyatt and Kasey hustled past the trooper, and they followed the medical staff. Wyatt watched the team work on Fassel as his EKG showed a flat line.

Kasey turned to Hughes. “What happened here?” she asked.

Hughes shrugged. “We were talking when he started choking,” he said.

Wyatt bent down by the bed and picked up something. He stuffed the item into his pocket. He rushed over to Kasey and took her by the hand. “We need to go,” he said. “Now.”

Kasey followed Wyatt back into the hallway. “What is going on?” she asked.

“When I fell to the floor before, I did it on purpose,” said Wyatt. He removed the item from his pocket. “I knew that Hughes was up to something, so I left my cell phone in there with the camera’s record button on,” he said.

Kasey smiled. “Nice move, MacGyver,” she said. “Play it.”

Wyatt was about to play the recording when the medical staff came out of Fassel’s room. Wyatt stopped a nurse. “Excuse me,” he said. “What happened to the patient in that room?” he asked. He put his phone back into his pocket.

“The man had a massive coronary event,” said the nurse. “I’m sorry, but he didn’t survive.” She placed a comforting hand on Wyatt’s left shoulder before moving away to join her colleagues.

Wyatt spotted Sheriff Hughes walking out of the room. “Sheriff, what happened in there?” asked Wyatt. “What did you do to him?”

Hughes stopped at glared at Wyatt. “Watch your tone, boy,” he said. “I didn’t do anything to him. We were talking and he suddenly seized up. The doctors tried to revive him, but they couldn’t.”

“Is that the official, police version?” asked Wyatt.

“That’s what happened,” said Hughes. “If you’ll excuse me, I now have a mountain of paperwork to do since this loser died on my watch.” He turned and stormed toward the exit.

Kasey pulled Wyatt closer to her. “Play your video,” she said. “I want to hear it.”

Wyatt and Kasey moved to a quieter area of the hospital. Wyatt turned on the recording. *“You little piece of crap. You should have died in that damn fire like you were supposed to.”*

“That’s Hughes’s voice,” said Kasey. Wyatt nodded.

“I did what you told me to do. What did you try to kill me? I wouldn’t have told a soul.”

“Fassel’s voice,” whispered Wyatt. Kasey nodded.

“You moron. You really thought I was going to pay you?

“I don’t need the money, Sheriff. Keep it. All of it. Just leave me alone.”

“I intend to leave you. All alone.”

“No! Stop! Stop!”

A loud beeping sound from the medical equipment drowned out the rest of the recording. Wyatt turned off the recording and he made sure it saved. “We have to go to the District Attorney’s Office,” said Wyatt. “Right now.”

Epilogue

The crowd at *Harold's* was loud and joyous. The eatery's regulars shared space with newcomers, and the occasional patrons. While most guests had to wait nearly forty minutes for a table, Wyatt James and Kasey Carpenter were ushered to a reserved table as soon as they arrived.

"This has never happened before," said Wyatt, as he and Kasey settled in their seats.

Kasey put her right hand on Wyatt's. "It must be the restaurant's way of thanking you," she said. "Enjoy it while it lasts." She smoothed a napkin over her lap. "Wow, it really is crowded tonight."

A waiter came to their table. "My name is Louie, and I will be your server tonight," he said. Kasey and Wyatt said hello. Louie leaned in closer to the couple. "Let me say that it is a true honor to serve you tonight. And the owner said that whatever you order for desert is on the house." He backed up. "What can I get for you?"

They gave Louie their orders and he rushed off to the kitchen. Wyatt bent toward Kasey. "I wanted to tell you that . . ."

Before Wyatt could finish, a woman in her late forties stopped at their table. "Excuse me," she said. "I'm sorry to interrupt, but can I get your autograph?" she asked. She handed Wyatt a pen and a small notepad. "My name is Georgina," she said.

Wyatt tried to smile as he quickly jotted down his name and hers. He handed the pad and pen back to Georgina. "Thank you," she said. "I want you to know that I think what you did was very brave," she said. "Well, enjoy your meal."

Kasey laughed as Wyatt rolled his eyes. She lifted her water glass. “Hail the mighty hero,” she said. She drank her water. “Admit it, you like the attention.”

Wyatt smiled. “It’s better than before when everyone hated me,” he said. He drank water from his glass. “Anyway, what I wanted to say was . . .”

A child ran over to Wyatt’s chair and nearly knocked him out of it. Wyatt carefully kept the boy from falling onto the floor. “Hi, I’m Charley,” said the boy. “My mom says that you are a real hero,” he said. “Is that true?”

Kasey smiled at the youngster. “Hi Charley. My name is Kasey and yes, Wyatt is a real hero. He is a firefighter, and he saves lives.”

“Wow, for real?” asked the boy.

A woman rushed over to the table. “I’m so sorry about this,” she said. She scooped the boy up and stood him on his feet. “Charley, you know better than to bother other people.” She looked at Wyatt. “I’m sorry, it won’t happen again.” She left with the boy in tow.

“Your fan club is growing,” said Kasey. She laughed again.

“I guess so,” said Wyatt. He took a breath and soldiered on. “Before anyone else stops by,” he said. “I want to thank you for everything you’ve done for me.” Kasey started to protest. “No, really. You’ve stuck by me through all this, and you gave me a job. And a new purpose. Thank you,” he said.

“You deserve it,” said Kasey. “You stood up for yourself, you proved your innocence, and you discovered what was really going on.” She raised her water glass again. “You are a true hero.”

A sudden hush fell over the crowd inside the restaurant. Wyatt looked over Kasey's shoulder at a television set in the bar area. The bartender turned up the volume. Wyatt pointed at the set with his eyes. Kasey turned around as a news report started.

"In the town of Penn Hills, a shocking case of corruption, arson, and murder," said a blonde television reporter. The woman walked through the center of town with the camera following her. "Earlier today, Penn Hills Sheriff Blake Hughes was arrested by state troopers for his alleged role in several arsons that occurred in this idyllic place."

"Idyllic place?" asked Wyatt. Kasey softly hushed him.

"Police allege that Hughes hired an ex-con named Brendon Fassel to set the fires as part of a plot to collect insurance money on the last property that Fassel allegedly tried to burn down. Hughes is a majority owner of the apartment complex and he stood to earn millions of dollars if his plan had worked."

The report shifted to footage of Hughes's arrest. "Hughes maintains his innocence and says that he looks forward to the opportunity to clear his name. Meanwhile, local firefighter Wyatt James . . ." A photo of Wyatt appeared on screen and the restaurant patrons cheered.

"Is credited with solving the case and bringing evidence of Hughes's guilt to authorities," said the reporter. "Deputy Colin James, Wyatt's brother, has been named interim Sheriff until next year's election."

The bartender turned the volume down. Several people came over and shook Wyatt's hand. Someone yelled out for Wyatt to speak. Others repeated the request. Wyatt looked at Kasey, and she smiled. "Say something, hero," she said.

Wyatt's face reddened. He stood up and the crowed quieted again. "Thank you. Thank you all for your support. It wasn't that long ago that I wasn't very welcome in Penn Hills, but now that the truth is out, I'm glad that's changed." Some murmurs in the crowd showed that they got his point. "I did not do this alone," said Wyatt. "I had the support of a wonderful woman named Kasey Carpenter. Stand up, Kasey," he said.

Kasey rose to her feet as the crowd cheered again.

Wyatt continued. "I'm happy that this situation has been resolved, and I'm even happier that the real perpetrator has been caught. I know many of us have been fearful since these fires started, but now we can rest assured that they will not continue. Thank you." The patrons clapped and cheered Wyatt as he sat down in his seat.

"Well said, Wyatt," said Kasey. "Maybe now we can get back to our lives."

The waiter arrived with their food. He placed their dishes on the table. "I want to let you know that the owner has changed his mind," said Louie. "Your entire meal is on the house."

"Thank you," said Wyatt. "Please give the entire staff our gratitude."

Kasey waited until the waiter left. "So, what will you do, now that this is over?" she asked. "Are you going back to Ohio?"

Wyatt slowly shook his head. "No, I've decided to stay here. With you."

Kasey's face beamed. "I'm glad to hear that."

"I have something for you," said Wyatt. He reached into his coat pocket and removed a small box. He handed it to Kasey. Her face flushed. "Go ahead, open it," he said.

Kasey's hands shook as she opened the box. She smiled when she saw the diamond necklace inside. "It's beautiful," she said. She carefully put it on.

"You look a little disappointed," said Wyatt. "Were you expecting something else?" he asked. He folded his hands and rested them on the table.

"I'm not disappointed," said Kasey. "More like relieved."

"How so?" asked Wyatt.

Kasey nodded. "I was afraid that you were giving me an engagement ring," she said. She exhaled. "I really care about you, but I don't think we are there yet." She leaned toward Wyatt and kissed him. "This gift is perfect."

"I'm glad you like it," he said. He cleared his throat. "Can you excuse me for a moment? I need to use the men's room," he said.

Wyatt rose and slowly walked toward the men's room. He was greeted by several people on the way, and he shook more hands. He reached the room and was glad that it was empty for the moment. Wyatt leaned against a counter and took another small box out of his coat pocket. He opened it and looked at the diamond engagement ring.

"I guess it is too soon for this," he said to himself. "It will have to wait." He put the box back inside his coat pocket. He washed his hands and dried them before exiting the room. Wyatt walked back to his table with a smile on his face.

He finally felt like he was home.

About the Author

Steven Donahue was a copywriter for TV Guide magazine for 14 years. His published novels are Amanda Rio (2004), The Manila Strangler (2013), Amy the Astronaut and the Flight for Freedom (2013), Comet and Cupid's Christmas Adventure (2013), Chasing Bigfoot (2014), Where Freedom Rings: A Tale of the Underground Railroad (2015), Solahütte (2017), Amy the Astronaut and the Secret Soldiers (2019), and Snow Angels (2021). Donahue is also the author of The Passion Cafe series. He lives in Pennsylvania with his wife Dawn, and an assortment of pets.

Made in the USA
Middletown, DE
09 January 2023